Game God Part I

ISBN-13: 978-1514127193

Printed in the United States

This book is dedicated to

Sara Davis, Cedric Davis, Big Cuz Squeek & Big Cuz Q,

Rest In Peace.

The setting of this urban slang fiction novel takes place in a greedy and drug infested part of Cleveland Ohio. Lives are taken and childhood friendships are destroyed. When up and coming Bud, Pete, and PW take to the streets to get a name for themselves, they find out the hard way that what goes around comes back around.

With the help of Larry an ex-pimp and recovering drug addict from the seventies Bud is on his way to the top. Bud has a plan to change the game by building an enterprise like no other but he starts to feel the ripple effect from the actions of the shady company he keeps, who fails to realize that street karma is real...

Struggling to keep his operation at the top. Bud finds his self in the middle of a fifteen year old territorial drug war between two dangerous cartels.

~Demetrius Hines

Chapter One

Community Ward 26 W. 82nd St, Money Avenue Cleveland, Ohio.

"Boy get yo ass out that window and come get this food before it gets cold!" shouted Granny D from the kitchen.

"Ok Granny!" responded Bud.

Bingo! He thought.

Expensive luxury sedans cruised up and down the avenue called Eight Deuce. The majority of these vehicles were owned by drug dealers.

The street was a residential area that housed wood framed homes with aluminum siding. The block attracted the undesirables of the neighborhood. Bud sometimes found himself daydreaming about the life. The life of a heavy hitter. From seeing the fame and fortune of others in the game caused him to want the same for himself. Bud never thought his dreams would become a reality.

Hearing his uncles' voices brought him out of his reverie. Big Mike, Bud's uncle was in the driveway of his mother's home working on a '73 Chevy Impala, with an all-white drop top. The exterior of the vehicle was candy apple green, with all-white alligator seats, sitting on twenty-four inch alligator rims. Big Mike was installing a music system into the vehicle. He was a low key cat who did whatever it took to get paid. Sometimes he would rob, steal cars, but selling drugs was his main hustle. His hobby was riding fast motorcycles.

As time went on he became very successful in the game. Big Mike was six-feet two; with a lazy left eye. His facial features were clean shaven. His heavy frame resembled the rap artist Biggie Smalls. His wavy hair was the result of endless brushing.

Bud walked through the hallway of his grandmother's house; the walls were painted earth tone colors. The aroma from the fried chicken permeated the house. As he passed through the hallway barefooted, he hit his small toe on the bathroom door.

"Mutherfucker!" he shouted... favoring his injured toe. As he was washing his hands he heard Granny D's voice.

"Boy come get this food, before it gets cold or your phatt ass uncle come in here and eat yo' shit up!

Bud ran down the steps. It was 1:45PM on a warm spring day in May. Bud kissed Granny D on the forehead, as he entered the kitchen.

"It smells good in here, I hope it taste as good as it smells." Bud stood over the stove inhaling the aroma of the chicken coming from the black skillet. Granny D washed her hands, and then dried them on her ten year old red and pink gown.

"I should whip yo ass for playing sick this morning, you and Pete being up all night! Your cousins should be in around three o'clock, make sure you save them some chicken and fries." Granny D said as she cleaned the spots of grease from the surface of the stove.

Granny D brought Pete and Lamika home from Alabama, seems like the right thing to do considering their mother was slipped PCP when Pete was just two years old… She hasn't been right since.

Before Bud could sit down he heard a loud boom. The base vibrating through the walls startled Granny D.

"I'm gone kill that boy!" Granny D said out of breath. Granny D worked the four o'clock shift at Health Works Hospital on the west side of Cleveland. She had three more years to go before she retired from the housekeeping department.

Bud walked through the kitchen vibing to the beats from PW's Chevy Impala. He could feel the heat suffocating the walls. He had to admit; his uncle was very experienced in the field of audio music. He grabbed his blue Cleveland Indians hat off his head and placed it on Granny D's favorite rocking chair. The Polo V-neck t-shirt complimented his 6' 3" frame like a model out of the GQ magazine.

Bud was more mature and tab bit smarter than the kids his age. His mother Cookie worked two jobs like the average single mother in the inner city. Big Mike's oldest brother Cortez was the reason Cookie did not want any more kids. His immaturity and lack of responsibility was too much during the time of her pregnancy.

Bud sallied through the backdoor. Putting his pro model hat over his dreadlocks. Big Mike and PW was smoking a haze blunt when Bud walked up stepping over the equipment Big Mike was using. Larry was sitting on a red milk crate separating the dirty towels from the clean towels. Big Mike saw Bud and said, "Nephew get the water hose out the garage for Larry."

"Thanks young blood!" He said balancing the EQ in the amp. Larry in his prime did numbers in the dope and pimping game back in the 70's. He put you in the mind of Floyd Money Mayweather... He ran with the best of the players from all over. Once the crack epidemic hit, his foundation crumbled. He still had a fly ass mouth, just fucked up without a bitch to pimp. No matter how hard Larry fell Big Mike kept him around. He made a living for himself by washing cars in the neighborhood

PW's phone rang. He inhaled the blunt flicking his phone open.

"Where you at?" He recognized the female voice,

"What I tell you about calling my phone like that. I told you about that goofy shit!" He hung up the phone; shaking his head; saying silly bitch under his breath.

PW, Pete and Bud were the same age. PW's whole family was murdered five years prior. His uncle fucked over some Jamaicans for two thousand pounds of weed not knowing he wouldn't live to spend a dime. PW came in from school to a brutal crime scene of his mother shot three times in the chest while taking a shower. The water was still running. His father's neck was slit from ear to ear while he was taking a nap on the couch. His twin sisters was raped and shot at close range. PW's uncle is still missing till this day.

Larry tapped Big Mike's shoulder.

"Always tricking and shit. My bitches would have had a field day with your cupcake ass. Shit lil' nigga you ain't getting no pussy like that!" Larry was putting the clean towels in the bucket.

PW was sitting in the passenger's seat of his car deleting numbers out of his phone.

"Who da fuck you talking 'bout Larry, I been getting pussy nigga!"

Meanwhile Lamika was in a stare down with Lulu from 20th trippin' over some cat named Tone from up the way. Lamika found her way through the row of wooden desks to where Lulu was sitting.

"I'ma beat yo ass after school bitch!" She said walking out of class as she put her hair in a ponytail.

"I knew your goofy ass was going to wet me up. Dope head ass nigga can't do shit right!"

"Big Mike what the fuck you got this stupid ass nigga around here fo?" Using his white tee to dry his face. Larry was too high to realize he never screwed the water hose on tight.

"Nigga fuck what you talking about you better have me and Big Mike's money for this wash and hooking up this music in this raggedy ass car!" He said screwing the water hose on tighter. Big Mike was focusing so hard on finishing PW's music; he didn't see his mother walk up on the car, playfully smashing his leg in the car door.

9

"I'm headed to work. Don't have all that traffic running in and out." His mother said as she dusted the lint from her work uniform. Bud walked Granny D to the bus stop.

His cell phone rang, "What's poppin?" TY was talking with the music blasting in Bud's ear.

"Damn nigga turn that music down in my ear like that!"

"My fault I was trying to see if you were out of school yet."

"Yea its cool call me when you get down the way."

Bud entered Mr. Bell's corner store on 84th and Money Avenue. As he walked past the old dusty potato chip racked, he slid his cell phone in his back pocket. He noticed the pinball machine sitting next to the chips was still out of commission for the last past ten years. Bud took a deep breath opening the cooler grabbing a cold Sunkist. *At least the pops are cold,* he thought to himself.

"How's your grandmother doing young man? I seen her getting on the bus the other day." Mr. Bell asked while ringing the items up.

"She holding up alright." Holding his chest from the strong pop. Mr. Bell fell silent for a second.

"Can I get three Cigarillos?"

"$3.75." Bud gave Mr. Bell a five dollar bill.
"Keep the change." Bud left the store feeling good about the opportunity the game bestowed for him.
Superior Avenue ran from downtown Cleveland to Cleveland Heights.

The environment always felt good to him and the smell of fresh BBQ filled the air. Bud loved to hear the sounds of cars riding up and down the street- As he looked around his neighborhood he smiled a nodded to the people he knew. He decided to walk to Northern High School on the corner of 79th. Bud was calculating the profit from his last pack and had it all mathematically figured out. He figured he could spend a thousand dollars on a pound of midgrade weed. Two grand for a quarter pound of exotic purple haze. Sell only ounces out of the midgrade for a hundred dollars a pop. Six hundred in profit off the midgrade. Sell only quarters out the purple haze for two hundred a pop maxing him out at eight hundred and ounces. He figured there was no need to invest in a lot of product.

Lamika had Lulu pinned down. Lamika's shirt was ripped off and her breasts were exposed to everyone to see .She had a patch of hair missing from the right side of her head.

"Told you I was gone beat that ass!" Smashing Lulu's head in to the ground. Lulu limped body laid lifeless as Lamika enforced strict punishment on her. Somebody from the crowd yelled, "She dead!" Bud pulled Lamika off Lulu just in time before the school security came.

"Fuck is wrong with you Lamika!" Pulling her by the arm. Running towards the cut on the side of the brick red building.

"Let me go!" She yelled out of breath. Still moving off her adrenaline she had forgot her shirt was ripped until Bud took off his and gave it to her.

"Fucking bugged out!" Reaching for his ringing cell phone.

"Fuck my phone at!" Patting at his pocket.

"What the hell you looking for?" Pulling the shirt over her head.

"I hear it but I can't find it." TY drove right passed Bud and Lamika. He found his phone on the fifth ring.

"Man my fault I couldn't get to my phone quick enough, you just rode past me turn around and pull on up Decker."

TY Pulled up in a four door Cutlass on 23" blades. The exterior was midnight blue with a sky blue rag top. The interior was the same color as the top.

"Watch the corner Lamika." Bud said.

"Yo where your shirt at?"

"Long story bruh!"

"What you trying to get?"

"Let me get what I always get." Handing Bud two fresh printed hundred dollar bills looking at Lamika. TY had a crush on Lamika from back in the day when they were younger, before he moved to the east side.

"Bud get at me." Putting his car in drive while looking at Lamika.

"What you looking at?" Lamika asked knowing Bud was looking at her ass jiggle back and forth in her fitted Baby Phatt jeans. They had sex a few times do to the fact they were not real cousins.

"You still like TY don't you?"

"He cool I would not mind spending some of his money."

"That's fuck up! You just want to spend a nigga money huh!"

"That's what's wrong with y'all broads, just be fucking with a nigga for his money. Soon as he gets locked up y'all ain't gone be around."
Talking to Lamika was like talking to a brick wall.

"Where your brother at?" Changing the subject.

"Ole girl from the bank came and picked him up this morning before we went to school." Pete was a natural at everything he did. Pete had a short stocky muscular upper body with a six pack. He never worked out a day in his life.

Bud and Lamika hit the front yard only to find Pete and Big Mike going back and forth.

"I know one of y'all stole my money out my stash. That's the second time this month somebody been in my room. I don't know if it's you or your sister."

"Nigga I told you already I don't have to steal from yo phatt ass!" Before Pete could finish Lamika ran through the screen door.

"Fuck you Mike phatt lazy eye ass nigga, it might be one of them nasty ass hood rats you bringing over here at night!"

What's next? Bud thought. He took a seat in the chair on the front porch and began emptying the guts of the cigarillos. His cell phone started ringing interrupting the family disturbance. It was Trina, his girlfriend of three years.

"What's up?" he said while disguising his voice while drying the blunt.

"Boy don't play with me. What other hoes you have around you?"

"Girl I'm just playing with you. I don't know if it's the water or the heat, but all y'all mutherfuckers going crazy!"

"I was just thinking about you." Putting his foot on the banister.

"What you about to get into?"

"I'm getting ready for work." She said as she was squeezing her two butt cheeks in her work denims. Her and Bud had a balanced relationship from day one.

"You want me to call off work? I just came off my period two days ago."

"Damn thirsty, you got to give that thang some time to breath. I'll rather see you at work anyway." Bud said blazing the blunt.

"We need to get you some help."

"I'm just fucking with you."

"Bud you smoking already? The day has not even started. You might need to check into rehab." she said smiling while tying her shoes up.

"You got jokes!"

"This the only way I can function. Weed ain't never did nothing wrong to me. Anyway I hope you saving your money."

"Boy don't get it twisted I probably got more money saved up then you."

"Oh you talking!" he said as he inhaled the blunt.

"What time is it?" he said blowing the smoke out.

"Don't be trying to rush me off the phone, I get the picture. I will call you when I get off work."

Soon as Bud hit the end button Big Mike went speeding out the driveway on his CBR motorcycle without a helmet on. Pete swung the door open angrily.

"Damn strong ass nigga!" An agitated Bud responded.

"Here hit the weed uptight ass nigga!"

"You look like you got something on your mind." He said as he passed the blunt.

"Man shit just ain't going my way, or moving fast enough for me. I gotta get my bag up bruh. It's time to take it to the next level out here you feel me?" he said inhaling the blunt.

Bud was rubbing his face with the back of his hand listening to an impatient Pete.

"I'm tired of wearing these same clothes every day."

"I feel you Pete. You can't rush success. These streets ain't shit to play with. The game god is a mutherfucker. If yo mind ain't right and you ain't got enough discipline to save your money you ain't got shit coming out here. It's all about the run my nigga."

"What you call getting money Pete?"

"Not living in this cooped up as house. I'm trying to live Bud, not tomorrow but today, right now my nigga. I'm tired of struggling. I want that big boy house with the CL out front. I'm on some fly shit these niggas faken' out here. Nigga ain't gettin' it like that and this I know.

"Pete sometimes you have to read between the lines. Everything that glistens ain't gold. I don't care who you are…. If yo mind ain't right these streets will gobble you up my nigga. It ain't about how much money you making it's about how much you can stack. Got damn nigga pass the weed ole hover ass nigga. Not only are you are smoking for free, but you smoking all the hazes up!"

Reaching for the blunt. "Like I was telling you look down the street. Tell me what you see."

"Nothing!"

"My point, you don't want to be thirty years old still out here on the corners bruh. Most of the old heads been out forever and still can't come up. Don't get me wrong the Deuces still do numbers. Just not like it did back in the day."

The Deuces was a million dollar block easy. You literally could make twenty to thirty thousand dollars a day selling rocks. Nothing but luxury cars. Dice games were like gambling on a Monopoly board. Every hustler from the Deuces is either dead or in the Feds. The conspiracy was so big it took down 170 people in ten cities and states.

Because Rock and Man-Man was trying to get on the airplane high. The niggas that lost their freedom behind Rock and Man-Man lack of experience in the drug game was enough to fuck up the average city or state.

DJ put Rock and Man-Man in a position of amenity and a life of crime. They were out of product for two weeks. DJ had just finished having a two hour conversation with Poppy his coke connect about stepping down from the franchise.

Over the years DJ had accomplished what a lot of drug dealers would have not accomplished in two life spans. His love for his two young protégés blinded him to the fact that they were not fully blossomed in the game at the level he played at. Not following his intuition, he knew they were too arrogant at the time.

They would ride Harleys in the winter with minks and gator boots. They kept new Range Rover, Benzes and Jags. Whatever you name they drove it. One summer they came through and blessed the strip, inside a big U-Haul truck filled with dirt bikes and four wheelers.

Fourth of July parties stayed going down. All the latest rap stars even a few movies stars would be in attendance.

The Deuces was jumping. Anybody who purchased dope in the early to mid-nineties purchased it from Rock or Man-Man.

Poppy was one ugly ass nigga from Puerto Rico. He was living LA. He sent the package to Cleveland three days ago. He was waiting on Rock and Man-Man to land at LAX Airport. Both renegades were taped up with two hundred fifty thousand apiece. The plane from Cleveland to LA left at 9:30pm.

DJ and Poppy sister Celena had met junior year at the University of USC. Celena introduced DJ to her brother and it was on and popping from that day on.

DJ knew what time the plane landed in LA
He himself had taken that trip many of times.

They arrived at Cleveland Scout Airport at 8:30pm.

"Call me when y'all land at LAX." DJ told Rock and Man-Man while they were getting luggage out the back of DJ's Range Rover. DJ had a funny feeling since he woke up that morning. Before entering the airport Man-Man told Rock to blaze up the half of blunt they had left.

Flight A19 Cleveland to LA was boarding. Man-Man was the first one through the metal detector. As soon as Rock went through, *Beep...Beep....Beep.* Man-Man eyes got big as hell. Turning around in shock to see his right hand man bringing unwanted attention. Rock heard the sound of the metal detector his heart skipped a beat. Two airport employees were walking by gate A19. One was a middle aged black man. The other was an overweight white female in her early 50's.

"Go back through!" the black employee said.

"It might be your belt." Man-Man said. Taking off his belt didn't work. *Beep .... Beep ... Beep,* same result.

Rock was starting to panic. Patting his chest and searching his pants pocket he somehow revealed the money that was taped to his right leg. The old lady relieved herself from her duties.

"Where that lighter at?" A tensed Rock finding in his lighter in his fifth pocket of his Tommy Hilfiger jeans.

Successfully clearing the metal detector. Not knowing it would be the start to one of the biggest drug conspiracy in years.

The fifty year old employee entered Officer Hayes' and Officer Young's door out of breath.

"We have two young men about to board flight A19 headed to LA smelling like weed. One of the men has money taped to his leg. Every time he went through the metal detector it went off!"

"Radio dispatch! Hold flight A19 to LAX FBI order!"

While Rock and Man-Man was getting seated, they were laughing and joking about what just happened at the metal detector.

"Man my heart still beating! Feels like my shit about to jump out my chest!" he said wiping the sweat from his forehead.

"You almost pissed yo pants." Man-Man was laughing in tears.

"Need you two to step of the plane and follow us." Two federal agents said flashing their badges. The two agents led the two of them to a small conference room and strip searched them. Finding what they were transporting.

"Oh what do we have here?" said a red faced officer Young.

"You two bitches think y'all can smuggle money and drugs in and out of my airport!" Looking and rubbing his fingers through the money. Officer Hayes took the money but did not arrest them.

"Now get the fuck out of my airport you two low lifers!"

"Aye Bud you know Shanicka is having a party Friday night. You trying to go?"

"Yea I have to meet Trina when she get off work at the bus stop when she call. Other than that we definitely can make it happen." He said throwing the last of the blunt in the grass.

Chapter Two

Granny D was not in the house from work a good five minutes when the doctor from Get Rich Clinic called.

"Hello is this Ms. Dean? This is Ms. Clark; I'm a doctor at Get Rich Clinic. Your son was in a motorcycle accident. He has suffered a mild concussion and has some swelling on the right side of his brain."

"How long has he been under your supervision?" A concerned Granny D asked while taking a seat on the couch.

It's been About three hours. We will be keeping him overnight, If you like you are more than welcomed to come here to see him, and we will be transferring him in to a room shortly.

Bud mother Cookie picked him up earlier that evening. He so happen to be walking to the bathroom when he heard the phone ring.

"Hello?" The sound of Granny D's voice got his attention quick.

"Where your mother at? Your uncle was in an accident a few hours ago. Take her the phone!"

Bud could not go back to sleep. He tossed and turned all night thinking about the last time he seen his uncle speeding out the driveway. Mad at Lamika and Pete about his money. He could not believe that Granny D was going to send them back to Alabama at the end of the summer. If he would have never walked her to the bus stop he would of never knew what was about to happen in the months to come.

Soon as he dozed off his father Cortez was banging on the door continuously like a madman.

"Open the door bitch I know you hear me!"
At first he thought he was dreaming. Until he heard the front door open up.

Man this nigga got to be geeked. It's five in the morning, talking to himself putting his house shoes on.

Before he could get to the front door he witnessed his father hit his mother in the back of the head. He grabbed the glass candy dish off the dining room table and threw it in the direction of his father's head, just missing his target by inches, shattering the window in the door. Running after his father.

"Hit me like that dope head as nigga. Hounding him halfway down the street.

Bud found his mother still sitting on the floor with her blanket and her arms wrapped around her legs rocking back and forth weeping.

"It's gone be alright ma!" Bud said to his mother as he helped her to the bedroom.

Bud took a shower. He hit the front door of Northern High ready for whatever after what happed last night. Entering the cafeteria of the first floor Bud was complimented with a hug and a kiss from Trina. She always was right on time whenever he was feeling down.

The two lovebirds had first block math class together for three years in a row. The day went by fast. After school he called his weed connect to re-up.

Pete ran game on one of his older females so he could use her car to go to Randall Park Mall. Bud liked shopping at Flex Collection and Heights Blue Fashion. Bud ended up coping a pair of Air Max 95. His cell phone started ringing while he was inside Footlocker paying for his shoes. It was Trina reminded him she was about to get off work.

"Who car y'all in." Turning the heat on.
"Girl what's wrong with you it ain't cold outside!" Pete shaking his head. Pete pulled up to Grubba Sea Food on 3rd in Bankston. Bud ordered a three catfish scampi dinners.

Chapter Three

The party was in full swing by the time Bud and Pete walked in. Bud was shocked to see how many people actually showed up to a house party. They both had one thing on their mind and that was getting their product off. They played the back wall so they could see everything going on around them. Pete never leaves home without his glock 40.

They rolled up two blunts to get the weed heads' attention. Pete had powder and pills. Bud had the haze.

"Pete blaze up."

"Damn she fine!" he said passing Bud the blunt. It did not take long for them to turn Shanika house party into a trap house.

"Well ... Well ... Well if it isn't Ms. Basketball herself." Bud said eyeing Shanika. He had to admit it Shanika was fine. This was the first time seeing her dressed like a lady instead of her basketball uniform. She had on a red fitted Bebe dress, with some red Andrew Marc pumps. Her high yellow skin tone was glowing.

"Oh Trina let you out tonight!" she said grabbing Bud's dick....

"She trusts you like that huh? So what brings you two this way?" Rolling her eyes at Pete.

"Damn! What I do to you?" he said inhaling the blunt.

Pete was feeling his self, "You know what brings me this way. Money and some of this fresh new pussy you got walking around in here!"

"You looking good your damn self!" he said passing Bud the blunt.

"Ain't she?" Playing the tag team game.

"I thought you were only into basketballs." He said blowing the smoke from the blunt in her face.

"Shiid from the looks of things she into bats and balls!" A laughing Pete said. Just in time her friend Erica walked up.

"What up Bud?"

"What up Pete?"

"Long time no see Pete, where you been hiding at?"

"You know me ma. I'm always on the go. But fo real fo real I been looking for you." He said moving in for the kill.

"Is it somewhere we can go talk?"

"Yea I'm up for it." She said grabbing Pete by the hand.

"Better watch him girl he might be scared, behave yourself lil' Peter."

"Ain't shit little about me."

"Not from what I heard." She said holding her two fingers up indicating the size of his muscle between his legs.

Pete pulled out a bank roll of all hundreds.

"Get your mind out the …" He caught his self before he said something he did not want to say.

"I didn't know you had it in you to throw a party like this."

"You niggas always doubting yo girl. I guess Trina got you so brainwashed you can't even see its bigger fish in the sea."

"What you got something against Trina?"

"Nope, I just want what she got." She said turning around making her ass clap.

"What you gone do when I put this pussy on you."

"You better calm down before you get what you're looking for."

"You smoke?" Passing her the blunt he asked. Grabbing the blunt she inhaled it like it was some midgrade. She was choking trying to find her breath.

The door swung open and PW walked in dressed to impress. He had on all-black Gucci cashmere and felt sweater with some stone washed black Gucci jeans and some all-black Gucci tennis shoes.

Shanika walked off to get something to drink. Trina's cell phone went dead two hours ago. She called Bud five times from her boss' office phone.

Bud knew Trina hated getting on the bus at night by herself. Soon as she came outside the RTA was pulling off. Sitting inside the bus stop was two junkies shooting dope when she walked up.

PW followed the weed aroma from the blunt where Bud was at. He came straight to the wall where he was posted at.

"Young Bud what up bruh?"

"What's poppin."

"How long you been here"?"

"About two hours. Me and Pete came."

"Where he at?" he asked looking Bud up and down.

"You already know."

"Damn nigga you dressed to impress!"

"Let me find out you fucking my hoes nigga. How y'all get here?"

"We walked." Bud said with confidence.

"Nigga y'all walked, quit playing. All that money you making yo tight ass won't buy no car nigga, you trippin."

Bud was feeling what PW was saying plus the haze had him zone.

"I know you don't want your peoples to find out you're hustling, but yo name is ringing bells in the hood bruh. Come fuck with a nigga its money to be made out here."

"You and Pete trying to kick it with a big dawg or y'all have to be in when the street lights come on?"

Bud looked at his phone. He had five missed calls. None of the calls were from Trina's cell phone.

He knew what time she got off work. He paid it no mind.

"Club Bottom Line jumping tonight. I usually fall through around one. You and Pete can roll if y'all want."

"That's what it is then. Let me sell the rest of my sacks and find Pete."

"How many sacks you got left?"

"Bout ten."

"Don't even trip; I'll buy em from you. Come to think about it my mans Matt from the west side selling a Honda accord and a '71 Cutlass already done up. All it need is some rims. He got jammed up fucking with TY hot ass."

"TY that used to stay behind us?" Bud asked.

"Yep!"

"That's crazy!" *I just sold that nigga some weed yesterday,* he said to his self.

"I just seen TY." Bud said not telling PW the whole story.

"Well you better watch that hot ass nigga."

"Well let me go find Pete so we can get up out of here."

Finding his way through the house. He seen Shanika eating some chicken and fries.

"Yo Shanika show me where the bathroom at." She showed where the bathroom was at alright. As soon as she showed him here the bathroom was, she pushed him inside, giving him a professional head job, looking him in his eyes seductively. The weaker his knees became the more skillful s her grip became on the tip of his bell head forcing him to let out an uncontrollable moan. She kept sucking until his little man became hard again. Bud could not resist her head game was too much for him not to dive into the pussy.

"You like this daddy?" While licking his rod up and down real slow, massaging his balls with his hands.

"Put it in Bud she nice and wet for you!" She said seductively.

Bud wasted no time injecting his rod deep in her guts.

"Umm Bud!" She whispered when his unprotected penis entered her Earth.

She bit down on her bottom and closed her eyes from the feeling. Bud has her pinned over the sink,

"This what you want?" Making his penis rubbed the right side of her walls. Every time his penis rubbed her wall it sent a sexual wave throughout her body. What turned Bud on more was the way her pussy lips swallowed his rod every time he penetrated.

"Ahh Ahh Ahh! Bud beat that pussy daddy! You like this wet pussy! Hit it harder I'm about to cum!" Letting out a loud moan that could be heard throughout the whole house.

Bud pulled out just in time, letting his future kids release all over her butt cheeks. This was Bud's first time fucking somebody that squirt when they cum.

"Trina don't fuck you like that!" Cleaning his penis off with hot soapy rag.

"Make sure you use that number." She said before closing the bathroom door.

Soon as Bud hit the hallway he heard yelling coming from the room at the end of the hall.

"Somebody help me! Get off me!"

"Shut up bitch!"

Bud put his ear to the door.

"Stop Pete!"

"Fuck that you going to give me some pussy!"

Bud busted through the door. "Pete what the fuck you doing! Erica you alright? Put your clothes on."

"Your cousin tried to rape me after I told him his dick was little and I didn't want to have sex with him!" She balled up on the edge of the bed crying.

"I know you scared, please don't tell nobody about this." Reaching in his pocket peeling off five crispy hundred dollar bills.

"I know five hundred isn't enough for how you feel, but it's the best I can do."

She ran straight to the bathroom.

"Pete what the fuck is wrong with you! So you taking pussy now huh bruh? Shit done got that serious you have to take some pussy, pussy she was about to give you. Nigga you out rabbit ass mind!" Bud was at a loss for words.

Bud spotted PW by the front door.

"Where we going?" Pete asked.

"Don't worry about it we ain't going to jail." A disappointed Bud said walking toward the car shaking his head.

Hopping in through the drop without opening the doors. PW pulled out a box of Cigarillos.

"Bud find us something to listen to." He found T.I.'s latest CD *Trap Music*. He put it on track number seven, *Burning Dro on Twenty Fours.*

"Pete you look like you mad about something." Looking at Pete through the rearview mirror.

"Yea I am! This nigga just fucked up my play for the night!"

"Nigga you better be glad I came in there when I did. You almost fucked your play up for the next ten years, thirsty dick ass nigga!"

"Fuck wrong with you two niggas man? It's Friday night, you niggas about to blow my high with all that yelling and shit! Relax grab that Grey Goose from underneath the seat. Pete hit that shit nigga. Here blaze the weed Bud, now relax both of you lil' niggas We about to hit the Flats, hit the club blow some money, fuck with some hoes and get our shine on." PW said putting the car in drive.

PW had the heavy Chevy wide open. *Boom ... Boom ... Boom* the base was knocking. The 24" blades was choppin' hard. Every time he mashed on the gas you could hear the motor work through the exhaust system. The night lights always seemed to enhance the candy paint on any car. PW's paint job under the city lights was like looking a piece of green Jolly Rancher fresh out the wrapper.

They were shining hard coming down Saint Clair Avenue. *Boom ... Boom ... Boom.* Seem like the bass from the music captivated their floss. The city always came alive around twelve at night. Cleveland night life on the weekends was always like a car show. By the time they hit E. 9th Street downtown traffic was bumper to bumper, candy paint everywhere.

It had to at least be about forty to fifty cars on rims in one line coming across the bridge that separated the east and west side of the city.

It was a female dancing on the hood of a candy red 1971 Chevy SS with all-white rally stripes sitting on some offset 22" rims. With the red brake covers. He had all-white swivel seats. His partner in the passenger seat was hanging out the power hole. Shorty looked like she was dancing in a strip club on the hood of the SS.

Club Bottom Line was jumping hard when PW pulled up. Pete was drunk as hell. He was standing up doing the shoulder lean in the back seat, waving a towel around in the air.

"Nigga I'm telling you its show time." He said jumping up and down. Bud felt like he had fifty stacks on him. The scene by the front of the club looked like a video shoot. The line was long. Since PW was a regular they got in free without getting searched. Preceding straight to the bar. The male ratio was 50:1.

As soon as they hit the bar, Pete ran into Black Tone from Longwood projects. Him and Black Tone did a Juvenile bid together.

"What up boy long time no see?" Black Tone asked.

"Can't complain, shit has its ups and downs. But other than that she booming around the way."

"How you holding up on your end? Last time we talked the ball was bouncing in your favor."

"Yeah bruh you know me I stay hitting them hard. I been in and out of town tearing the streets of PA up?"

"What you drinking? It's on me."

"Oh yeah I almost forgot, Black Tone this my people Bud and Pete. We about to mingle you more than welcomed to join if you want."

"Good look on the bottle, I came with my peeps. I so happen to see y'all walk in, just wanted to pay my respect." Giving PW dap before he walked off.

PW, Pete and Bud walked over to the picture booth. It was some attractive broads flirting with Bud and PW. They held down the picture booth for thirty minutes. Females they didn't know were taking pictures with them. Club Bottom Line was packed wall to wall when the DJ started playing *Swamp Nigga* by Master P. The club was intensified. Everybody was mean mugging niggas bitches. PW was standing on the pool table singing the words to the song with two Moet bottles in his hands.

Niggas from the south rock gold in they muthafucking mouth. PW pouring out Moet.

"I told you." Pete said passing Bud the blunt.

"I feel you my nigga." Bud observing the club scene. Shit was moving in slow motion.

"What up!" A female voice taking him out his zone.

"What's poppin!" Bud said slurred voice, turning the Moet bottle upside down.

"Who you came here with?" Inhaling the blunt.

Some cat walked passed and bumped Pete on purpose.

"Damn nigga say excuse me?" Pete grabbing the Moet bottle of the table.

"My fault nigga!" Mean mugging Pete.

"Damn ma turn around let me see that ass in them jeans." Bud asked.

PW had the spotlight on him. *All About the Benjamins* came on. Pete hopped on the table with PW and started throwing money. Some cats from the other side of the room threw a bottle at PW. The bottle just missed him and hit an innocent female in the back of the head, the scuffle was on. Somebody stole on Pete dazing him hard. Bud turned around just in time before dude hit Pete again, busting the bottle over his head.

"Yeah bitch ass niggas hit me like that!" *Boop* Somebody hit Bud dropping him with one punch. PW jumped off the table on old boy back who hit Bud. People they did not know were helping them fight. Black Tone and his crew came out of nowhere. Soon as Bud got back to his feet somebody hit him again. Black Tome and Pete was stumping some dude out under the pool table. The fight spilled out into the front of the club. That's all Pete wanted was to get to the car. PW was right behind him. Pete grabbed his glock and PW grabbed his Tech 9 from under the seat. *Boom Boom Boom* The shots from the Tech 9 spit out rapidly. The crowd started moving real quick. PW was laughing while letting the t Tech rip while spiting blood from his busted lip. *Tat Tat Tat Tat* You could hardly Pete's gun while he was shooting. Hitting the gas station on 55th and Woodland right behind the projects.

The Marathon gas station always draws the crowd after the clubs let out on the weekends. The third district police was already in position before the crowd and traffic got too thick. PW pulled across the street in Rally's parking lot. It was two cars parked there already. One was a candy root bear box Chevy with peanut butter interior. Sitting on 24" all gold spokes and the other vehicle was a two door GMC Yukon with a midnight blue paint job, with all-black tint and a Chevy light up sign in the grill with step up bars. Slim's truck was in the top ten in the city easily, sitting on 26" deep dish Giovana rims.

The females were out and the Marathon was doing what it do best. There was no need to get gas. It would have been a waste of time. If the police was not moving traffic then it was not going to get moved.

"Man this bitch going hard!" PW said closing his car door.

"Let's go get something to eat."

"Pete who the hell eat food from the Marathon at this time of night, yo stomach gone be through." PW said while observing the traffic.

"This shit crazy you got everybody outside in the hood, plus everybody who wants to be a part of the hood, I know they strip rocking. Too much traffic always bring the fiends out." Bud said standing up inside the car to stretch.

"Shiid! Fuck the strip. You know how many niggas get robbed out here on the side of that gas station going to take a piss. Look how dark it is. In the daytime you can see the cut that leads to the back of projects but not at night. See look, look at ole boy y'all drunk as hell stumbling to the side of the gas station as we speak." Pete said shaking his head, knowing how vulnerable some niggas be in the morning after they leave the club.

"Pete you stay ready for a lick."

"Ain't no question. Police don't give a damn about nobody taking a piss, it's too much other shit to worry about. Two lines of cars in the middle of the intersection trying to get in the gas station. You got all the traffic coming from Jack's Sports bar on Cedar Rd. All the traffic coming from downtown and the Flats coming to this one gas station. Look the line out the door. On top of that they selling food. To take the cake you got niggas leaving their cars running trying to holla at some hoes. It is 4:30 in the morning, perfect time to catch one of these niggas slipping."

"Aye man let's go get something to drink." He said tapping PW on the back.

"I got cotton mouth!" He said wiping his mouth with his hand.

"Hold on bruh, I don't mind going over there with you. We have to be in and out. I only have three bullets left." He said double checking his glock.

"We got to make this shit quick. Don't be in their trying to talk to every chick you see either PW." A nimble Pete said.

"Man let's go nigga." PW said walking toward the thick traffic that clogged E. 5th street.
PW was not listening to shit Pete said. It was four females inside a red four door Dodge Neon. PW was all inside the driver's window.

"Bud look she ain't got no panties on bruh!"

"I just told you about that shit!" Pete said moving his right hand as he talked. PW ran and caught up with a laughing Bud and a delirious Pete.

"Aye Pete!" he said putting his arm around his neck.

"Aye my nigga you know what, smell this!" he said putting his two fingers in Pete face he stuck inside ole girl's juice box.

"Man what the fuck wrong with you!" he said pushing PW. PW was laughing hard as hell. They were in and out in no time. Soon as they stepped back into society Bud seen the one female he was talking to inside the club. This time she had her two sisters with her.

"What a coincidence it seems like you following me ma." Bud said.

"What is your name?"

"My name is Lena for the second time." It seemed like Lena was bad luck because Pete never saw ole boy who bumped him in the club earlier. Pete was hitting the bottom of the apple juice bottle when a hard right hand hit him in the jaw. The impact from the punch forced Pete to stumble into Lena. His Mr. Pure apple juice bottle hit the ground. Pete came back up shooting his last three shots *Boom Boom Boom.* People started running. All you could hear were police sirens and the sound of humanity hitting their car horns. The scene looked like the scene off *Boys in the Hood.*

Bud, Pete and PW was sprinting toward the car. PW dropped the keys two times in his lap before he got the car started. *Errrrrr* ... Both back tires burning rubber from the four ninety six rear end. Speeding toward 55th and Woodland. He almost crashed into a parked police car that was parked in front of the post office. Bullets were chasing them just missing their heads.

"Watch that police car!" Bud said ducking down in the front seat. Making a left on Bundy, PW disregarded the stop sign doing eighty up the wrong way of the one way. He hit 65th and Quincy with his lights off. He did not realize his lights was off until he came flying past the graveyard on Central Avenue. It was two police cars sitting inside the plaza on 79th and Cedar flashing their lights on two dope heads sitting inside the bus stop shooting heroine. Soon as PW hit the left hand turn onto Cedar the call came across the scanner.

"We have a shooting in progress location the Marathon gas station on 55th and Woodland."

Hearing the sirens PW hit the gas even harder. He pulled into the back of Granny D's driveway happy to still be alive after what just transpired with the devil of the streets.

"Man that shit was crazy back there bruh! It don't take no time to get into some shit." PW said hitting the wood grain. Pete was hanging over the side of the car vomiting.

"Yo what the fuck you sick nigga?" Bud asked turning around to see what the hell was wrong with Pete.

"Bruh you better take yo sick ass in the house." PW said laughing at Pete.

"Hope you ain't been going raw on them hoes out here, because that shit that just happened we go through that shit every day!"

"Fuck you talking about I do this shit. I told you nigga I had too much to drink. I put in more than both you nigga." He said spitting the rest of the vomit out of his mouth.

"Why you talking I hope you didn't get that shit on the side of my car!"

"Nigga fuck you!" Pete said gazing into the constellation.

Larry knocked on the door five times before Granny D came to the front door. The smell of fresh fried bacon permeated through the air.

"Who is it?"

"It's me MS. D!"

"Come on in Larry. I been waiting on you all morning. I will meet you in the backyard. I have to flip this bacon."

Granny D left out the back door to find PW, Pete, and Bud sleep inside the car.

"Look at these Fools!" Larry said while opening the driver door.

"Child leave them kids alone." Granny D said with her hands on her hips. Larry was tapping PW pockets when he woke up to the sound of Granny D's voice

"What the fuck you doing with yo thirsty ass?" PW said pushing Larry out the way with his left arm.

"Don't you got some work for this old nigga to do Granny D?" PW said getting out the car.

"Y'all must of had a rough night for y'all to fall asleep in this here pretty car. Bud your grandfather had a car like this when we was younger." She said bending down to grab the garage door handle.

"I was watching the news this morning. All kinds of bad stuff happened last night. Some lil' girl got raped, it was two shootouts. One was in front of the club in the Flats the other one was at the gas station. I don't know what this world is coming to. I'm sure is glad y'all ain't have nothing to do with that stuff."

Bud took a deep breath and looked at Pete before going into the house to run him some bathwater. Bud put his cell phone on the charger. He called Trina from the house phone, still no answer. *She might be still sleep,* he said talking out loud.

Pete walked in his sister's room and jumped on the bed, pulling the covers back.

"Pete I'm tired get out!" she said with slob all over her face. PW was in the kitchen eating some pancakes and bacon that Granny D had cooked.

Bud closed his eyes and let the hot water suffocate him. He kept replaying last night events from the house party, to the club then the gas station shootout and how close he came to death. He was listening to Pete and PW through the vent talking about last night

"Nigga you seen me when I jumped on ole boy back who hit Bud? I damn near killed his ass!" PW said stuffing his face.

"That nigga hit me so hard at the gas station; I'm still looking for that nigga."

"I thought you were talking about the nigga who dropped yo ass in the club!"

"I can't even front I thought you was done bruh. That shit had me so mad I started hitting bitches too!" PW said walking to the sink.

"That shit happened so quick. Did you see how quick I got back up doe? That nigga Bud is one nigga I got to have with me any time I hit the club or the bar. That nigga act like he been in a hundred bar fights!"

"Shiid some nigga made him kiss the paint to!" he said turning the water on in the sink.

"Since you seen everything what the fuck was you doing while we was fighting?"

"Naw all jokes a side right now, you think Granny D will let me take a shower, I got some fresh clothes in my trunk."

"Naw why the hell you ask that dumb as question?" Pete asked pouring him something to drink.

Bud was feeling some kind a way about Trina not calling or answering her phone. He went and set on the porch with Lamika, Larry and Granny D.

"You see this Larry?" Granny D asked looking at Dave get dragged halfway down the street by a dope head before letting go of the car. She was mad as hell.

"Every day same people doing the same shit. Dave was out here selling drugs before Mike was and he still out here on this corner. Nothing but the devil he is always at work 24/7 he never sleeps."

"All these lil' kids think it is cool to sell drugs, rob people and disrespect the women. They killing them self and the community at the same time. Last week they had a meeting about closing some of the public schools in the inner city. It's a sad state of mind that our people are in as a whole. Hand me that trash bag Larry. These lazy ass kids throw trash down and keep walking without a care in the world. When I was younger your next door neighbor could beat your behind."

"Not no more." Lamika said looking at her finger nails.

"I know damn well you can't. That's because y'all too busy smelling yo on ass." PW came out the door just in time.

"Bud you rollin' or you staying here?" PW asked walking down the steps.

Once they hit the west side bridge Bud already knew where they were going. PW stopped in the West 28th projects to holla at Mario. The West 28th projects were built on the bank of the Flats. They pulled onto a residential side street off of West 130th. He pulled into a wood framed house with a brick red driveway. Before they could get out the car a short stocky dude came out the side door. It looked like he was mixed with black and white. He had a clean bald fade and his style of dress was of a dope boy. He had on some all black Polo sweats with some throwback Bo Jackons on.

"PW what's good fam. I been waiting on you for about three days."

"You know how shit is. A nigga say one thing but the streets make you do another thing, but I'm here now, so what's good? What you got for me? Matt this my mans Bud I was telling you about."

Matt opened the garage. Bud fell in love with the beauty of American muscle. The '71 Cutlass was in show room condition. He lifted up the hood and chrome was everywhere. 454 big block chrome intake and chrome headers. The exterior was pearl white. The interior was factory peanut butter bucket seats. The crazy thing about it was it was a stick and still had the factory radio in it.

"How many miles she got?" Bud asked walking around the car.

"Start her up." Hearing the sound of the motor, Bud knew it was a lot of money tied up into this car.

"God damn what the hell you got under da hood bruh?" Bud asked looking at the exhaust system.

"Man this bitch running. How many miles she got Matt and how much you want for this car bruh?"

"You know I ain't trying to get that much since you fuck with my mans. I'll let you get it for about four stacks. Give me five and I even got a Honda Civic out front you can get both of them. Give me five stacks and they both yours."

"Why you selling these cars so cheap?"

"Man long story bruh. Fucking with hot ass TY. He called me one day trying to get four and a half ounces of soft. He tells me to meet him at the old skating rink on Ridge Road. When I get there police was everywhere. Shit cost me seventy five hundred dollars in lawyer fees. Man fucked my whole flow up. I'm gone deal with that nigga when all this shit blow over, so right now everything must go until I bounce back."

"Damn that's fuck up. TY used to live down our way back in the day!"

"Yea I know, that what PW was telling me. That rat ass nigga ain't right." Matt said shaking his head. You could see the hate in his eyes and his body language.

"I only have two stacks on me right now. PW let me get three bands until we get down the way."

"I can do that foe you bruh."

"Matt I will meet you Monday morning at the license bureau out Blue Block Heights to get the paperwork right."

PW and Bud were on their way back to the east side when Mr. Clark called his phone.

"Hello?" Bud answered turning the radio down. He could hear the chafing in his voice.

"How far away are you from my house?"

"Bout 15 minutes, that's cool with you Mr. Clark?"

"Yea I will be waiting on you."

"PW take me to Trina's house something do not sound right. Last night she didn't call my phone when she got off work last night."

"Everything cool bruh don't trip."

They pulled into Trina's driveway. Mr. Clark was sitting on the steps with his face buried in his hands. His eyes were the color of flames.

"PW I will hit you when I leave from here." He said giving PW dap before getting out the car.

"Mr. Clark you alright?"

"Last night two dudes raped Trina!" Letting his emotions drip down his face.

"At the bus stop last night. Somebody found her around two o'clock last night. She was unconscious when they found her laying inside the bus stop."

"I had a few missed calls last night. None was from Trina so I thought that you or her mother was going to pick her up. I always met her at the bus stop every Friday night." He said taking a seat next to her father.

"I just left from buying her a car that's where I was coming from when you called. So she won't have to catch the bus no more. What the fu...!" Catching his words that he was in loss of.

"How didn't nobody see nothing?" Bud asked scratching his head.

Bud walked inside Trina's hospital room. She was sleep from all the medicine they had her on. Just to envision Trina looking like that made Bud breakdown instantly. He could see the fatigue on her mother's face. She gave him a hug as soon as he entered the room. He felt it was his fault because he was not there.

"It was my fault!" he kept saying in tears holding on to Mrs. Clark. He took a seat next to the bed looking at the bruises she suffered to her head and her face were unbearable. He grabbed her hand and held it tight. *How the hell could I save Erica from getting raped by Pete and nobody was there to help Trina,* he thought.

"Do you two mind if I have a minute alone with her?"

"Trina I'm sorry bae. I should have been there." He said rubbing his finger through her hair.

He did not know she was woke until she squeezed his hand. She had a tear running down the left side of her face.

"It's not your fault." she said in a low pitched voice. Trina was trying to smile, but the swelling in her top lip prevented her from smiling.

Mr. and Mrs. Clark watched from the doorway in tears seeing Bud express his emotions to their only daughter. Mrs. Clark was so effusive looking at Trina mourn like she was.

"It's okay Bud, things happen. I have something to tell you."

"What is it?" he said lifting his head up.

"I'm pregnant, three weeks pregnant."

The news was mind blowing to him because he was not expecting for her to say that.

Bud stayed overnight with her and they talked like best friends getting to know each other. They stayed up all night watching TV. Bud called Cookie to come pick him up. It was the first time his mother had sat down with Trina's parents. The ride home was self-contained until his mother broke the silence.

"I talked to a good friend of mine; he said he can get you into Barber College next semester for half price at the Lake Turn Up Barber College since you always talking about you want to cut hair." She said turning into the driveway. He went straight to his room and counted his money. He had to pay PW back the three grand. That was the first thing on his mind. He called PW.

"Yo what it do bruh you alright?"

"Yea, come pick me up from my mother crib." PW pulled up in an all-black Chrysler 300, no tint and thirty day tags."

"Damn nigga that's how you feel!" he said hopping inside the car.

"Here go yo few stacks I had got from you. It's all there nigga ain't no need to count it." Bud said adjusting the seat.

"Shiid nigga I always count mine nigga!" PW said putting the car in drive.

"Call ole boy Matt." PW cut him off.

"Relax that's my mans. Matt is all business!"

"If that's your word then I'm going to hold you to that."

PW blended in with traffic pulling up to T-Man's gambling spot on 10th Wale. PW wasted no time placing his first bet. The gambling spot was filled with all different hustlers from all over the city.

He placed a fifty dollar bet to get a feel for the dice game. Lil' Man from Lakeview rolled trips on the come out. He had a mean pad roll. The weed smoke was so thick that it looked like fog. The smell of fried fish and weed soaked all in your clothes is a hell of a smell.

It was two cats gambling on the play station. They were playing NBA Live for five thousand a game on the flat screen with a small crowd around them.

It was a card table off to the back of the house inside a small room, they was playing poker for a thousand dollars a hand. T-Man was getting phatt off the cuts from the dice game, card game and the play station game. It was a win win for him. Lil' Man rolled *3-3-4* four other people fell to his point. PW was the last one to shoot. He rolled *4-5 -6* on the first roll.

"All shit y'all den fuck up let a young nigga like me get the bank! I'm about to break these nigga. Bud give me five hundred. Bank is a stack, whoever getting down put your money on the ground we only paying what we see!" He said tying his shoes up tighter.

"Bud watch these slick ass nigga bruh. I'm gone shoot. You gone collect. Here T-Man, I'm gone pay you for the next five come outs."

Within ten minutes he broke the whole house. He broke the house for a quick eighteen stacks.

"Did you see Rob face when he fell to the dice for the seven stacks man he could of shitted on his self. I know that was his last seven stacks in life. He always has his last or all his money on him." PW said putting his 357 back under the seat.

"Now let's split this shit up. Nine stacks fo you and nine stacks fo me. Fuck with yo boy I'm gone always keep you around the money!"

PW took Bud back to the crib. He was feeling good he had just won nine stacks off of a five hundred dollar investment. He gave his mother a stack and put the rest in the orange Nike box underneath his bed. He put in the *Best of the Isley Brothers* Cd in. *I'll Always Come Back to you* floated throughout his small room. He collapse on the bed.

Chapter Four

Meanwhile

"Lay it down nigga! Shut the fuck up nigga! Hurry up duct tape his legs!" Starr said hitting the victim in back of the head with the gun.

"Where the money and the work? Pete asked aiming the 30/30 at the victim.

"Man I ain't …!" *Boom* … Pete hit em with a leg shot. Nutt was looking out the window when a police car rode pass hitting the brakes and stopping by the stolen getaway car.

"Po Po y'all! They just stopped in front of the house. I think they looking at the car. Man I hope they don't get out the car." Nutt said.

Starr kicked the victim three times in the leg where he was bleeding from, when he started yelling.

"Oh you trying to get the police attention nigga!" Pete said punching him in the stomach. The cop car sped off.

"I'm gone ask you one more time. Where the fuck is the money at? You out here flossin' hard nigga. We know you loaded." He said sticking the barrel of the gun inside his wound.

"Aright!" he yelled grimacing in pain.

"Aright … Aright! It's two duffel bags in the garage!" he said holding his hand up letting them know he had enough of their torture. The police car had pulled up next to the car again.

"Man this motherfucker back again, and he getting out!"

Pete came from the garage.

"Yea nigga!"

"Shut yo loud ass up nigga! Police just pulled back up!"

"Fuck you mean police just pulled up!" He said running to the window.

"Nutt you left the car running?"

"Yea I did! What you told me to do!"

"Look drag his ass off to the back of the house. Make sure you tape his mouth up!"

The police officer walked up on the windshield of the vehicle to see if the steering column was peeled. They heard two knocks at the door. It froze the whole scene inside the house. Pete looked at Starr and pointed to the door. The officer's knocks got more aggressive. Before he could knock again Starr opened up the door with her cleavage exposed.

"May I help you Sir?"

"Yea I was wondering do you know who car this is it has been sitting here for about ten minutes. Whoever car it is they left it running."

"That's Terry car, he took his little son in the house he always do that he ain't gone be satisfied until somebody pull off with his car." she said rubbing both her hands through her hair so the officer could get a good look at her breasts.

"Okay you have a nice day young lady." The police officer was too busy looking at Starr's breast that he did not see the blood that was on the floor or Starr pistol sitting on the table by the door.

"He gone! Hurry the fuck up let's get up out of here!" Starr said running to the stolen Chevy. *Errrrrr* ...

"Slow this bitch down Starr!" Nutt said throwing his ski mask out the window.

"That's how you get right nigga!" Starr pulled on a street that led to a dead end.

"Nutt you know what to do. We will meet you at the spot."

Starr was Pete down bottom bitch from day one. He met her at Euclid Shopping Center. She was a red bone with blond hair, pink lips and hazel eyes. She was strapped for her age. Pete was in love with her. They always hit licks together. Using her for bait made majority of the licks easy because the average cat getting money has one weakness, pussy.

Chapter Five

The Come Up

Bud woke up by the hard vibrant knocks of Pete consistent knocking on the door. Looking through the peephole he saw Pete's face.

"Yo what the hell you want?" he said opening the door.

"Yea nigga it's show time bruh."

"Hell you talking about? He said wiping the corner of his eye.

"Why the hell you got a book bag on for? All my years knowing you I ain't ever seen you with a book bag."

"Don't worry about the bag; it's about what's in the inside!" Pete said throwing the book bag to Bud.

"Fuck you looking at?" He asked unzipping the bag.

"Them crusty as feet. You too young to have feet like that. That's a damn shame yo feet look that bad!"

"Pete what the hell you want me to do with this shit?

"It's yours bruh! The whole bird and the ten stacks. From this day on ain't no more looking back. I want you to call PW and tell him to meet us on the Deuce."

"Bruh I still got weed."

"So what now you got weed and dope get right."

Pete came all the way up off his last lick. Five birds and eighty stacks. He gave Bud and Nutt a bird and ten stacks a piece. He gave Starr twenty grand. He was waiting to see PW so he could break bread with him.

"Bruh I ain't seen yo ass since we went out then all of a sudden you pop up with a bird and ten stacks. So much shit has been going on in these last few days. Trina got raped the night we went out."

"Get the fuck out of here, you for real the night we went out. So that's what Granny D was talking about. Somebody got raped at the bus stop. I wasn't paying that shit no attention what she was talking about."

With PW hustle hand and Pete extortion game, they opened up shop on the Wade park end on the Deuce, selling twenty dollar bust downs during the day and hundred dollar blocks at night. With Larry cooking the product he knew what all the smokers wanted. Straight dropping butta. It was a perfect location. Within weeks they had clientele from all over the community. The money was flowing in good, they only had one problem, and the product was getting low. Once they sold out, they took a trip to Niagara Falls. Interstate 90 East led them straight to the Holiday Inn on Delaware Avenue downtown Buffalo. Buffalo was Larry's old stumping ground from back in the day. The ladies wanted to go shopping at the Walden Gallery shopping mall before it closed.

Pretty boy Tone wanted to get his hair cut. Larry took him to Magic Legends Barber shop. The barber shop was home to some of the great legends in the game in the city of Buffalo. Trina being pregnant she had a taste for some fried rice. Larry took them to an upscale restaurant in the suburbs called Sho-Guns.

After eating they went back to their hotel rooms to get ready to hit club Groove. Larry was taking all day getting dressed. The ladies were starting to get impatient.

"Somebody go up there and get Larry? Te Te said using the mirror on the inside of her hand bag to put her lip gloss on.

Boom Boom "Larry open up my nigga what the fuck you in there doing?" PW asked.

"Hold on give me five more minutes."

"Alright we will be waiting on you in the lobby whenever you get done playing with yourself."

Larry was in the room in tears flushing the last of his crack habits down the toilet. Smoking crack he had lost everything. Bud reminded him of DJ so much to tell the truth he missed Man-Man and Rock. He remember the first day DJ brought them to the Deuce, from looking at them he could tell they was natural street nigga just how they carried their self in such aggressive environment they never back down from no body, they even had a few shootouts with the local police.

Larry so happened to be with DJ at the time when Rock called his phone sitting on Pookey's porch.

"We need to talk." Rock said.

57

"Talk about what? Poppy already told me y'all did not make it out there to LA. I have made millions of dollars doing business with Poppy. I gained his trust by being a man of my word and respecting the morals and principles of the game, something you two lack. I don't know what you two are on but I hope one of y'all is man enough to tell me what really happened and why y'all could not make it to LA. Either y'all got jammed up in Cleveland or in LAX airport."

All Rock and Man-Man phones were tapped. Hearing the static in the phone Rock looked at the phone kind of crazy but paid the static no mind.

"Look I will meet y'all at Lancer's restaurant in two hours." DJ hung up the phone in his face.

"I know them nigga got knocked Larry, at that airport!" Throwing his cell phone in the bucket of water that Larry used to wash his car with. Larry understood the game and how it was played and how much was to be lost if Rock and Man-Man got knocked fucking around.

DJ had reach kingpin status five years ago. He was serving drug lords from all over. He was making two million a week. Poppy kept A1 work. DJ never broke nothing down or stepped on anything. Money was never the issue with Rock and Man-Man. Poppy was a man of morals and principles. He told DJ he did not respect his two protégés being in charge of his drug operation, but he understood where he was coming from and how he felt about falling back from the game.

Larry and DJ was waiting at the bar eating scampi. Two federal agents were taking pictures from twenty feet away when Rock parked his vehicle. Man-Man hopped out the car first. They walked in and fused with Larry and DJ at the bar. The two federal agents set four tables back perceiving everything that was said and scene. No one talked for about five minutes. Larry went outside to smoke a cigarette.

"So what happen? Why y'all never made it to LA?" DJ was grilling Rock because he knew better. He molded him from day one to take over after he stepped down.

"Man we just was not feeling it bruh. You told us to follow our first mind and that's what we did."

DJ could feel the deceitfulness and the vibe from their lack of confidence in their story.

"So why nobody called me and tell me to call Poppy or to pick y'all back up from the airport?"

"We we wee we ra raan!" A stuttering Man-Man said.

"We ran into some females and got right."

"Come on now you gone run that weak ass game on me! Who the fuck you think you talking to!" A nonsensical DJ said slamming his hand into his plate.

The two agents bumped Larry on the way out.

"Damn say excuse me disrespectful mutherfucker!" Larry said throwing his cigarette butt to the ground. The middle aged agent turned around and flashed his badge.

"Tell your two friends thanks and if they want their money back tell them we would be more than happy to give them a job for their services."

When the elevator doors opened up they could not believe it was Larry. He had on wool twill coat with a detachable beaver collar cashmere silk bowtie, with a wool hound tooth trousers.

"Fuck y'all looking at! I told you lil' nigga I do this shit. Shit comes easy to a playa like me." Larry said walking out the front door of the Holiday Inn.

"Larry unlock the doors." Tete asked. He had forgot the keys up in his hotel room on top of that he locked his self out.

"Look at yo dumb ass can't do shit right nigga. You done washed yo ass and done forgot how to act and shit with yo funny looking ass!" PW said.

When Larry came back to the van, PW gave him a hug.

"You look good big homie. I'm proud of you my nigga stay clean."

"I have to make one stop before we hit the club." Larry said turning on Delaware Avenue. He pulled on Walden Avenue on the east side of Buffalo to find Big J a longtime friend he had met at one of Good Game player balls back in the day.

He hopped out the van leaving it parked in the middle of the street.

"Big J what's good!"

"Larry that's you? I be damn look at my nigga!" The two embraced.

"Boy it's been about ten years since I last seen you, how you holding up?"

60

"Well Big J, to be honest bruh I'm just now getting back right. These lil' nigga gave me something to live for again." He said pointing to the van.

"You know what they say; no matter how hard you fall you still have to get back up. I'm glad you stop by to check up on me man. Before you leave I have something for you to smoke on. You and yo lil' mans and nem." He gave Larry an ounce of dro.

Downtown Buffalo was totally different from downtown Cleveland. Everywhere you went or ate at; it always was a talented musician playing the saxophone with such passion. Majority of the musicians were playing for money to support their drug addiction. Some was playing because it was where they music came alive to them.

The VIP section of the club was well thought of from the setting to the color scheme. From the VIP room you could see the crowd down stairs but they could not see you. The strippers did not look like the average females. A lot of them were different nationalities. A few of the strippers looked like they were in college trying to make ends meet. Something about the club PW was not feeling tilt. This was his first time going to a club in another city. I guess not having his strap or the weed Big J gave them had him off his square.

When the club closed, Seneca Niagara Casino was the only place you could go to end your night. They played the Casino until daylight, so they could be the first ones in line to get on the boat that crossed over into Canada. They wanted get a close up of the waterfall. Niagara Falls was a waterfall that you could visit three times a year and still be intrigue with the natural beauty of Mother Nature and how the mist from the waterfall would hit your skin, or just how fresh the water smelled. The females felt like they were in the motherlands. They had never been outside the city, so to them seeing Niagara Falls was like the world to them.

Bud was so caught up at the height of the waterfall. The sound had him lost in the moment. Pete snuck up behind him and scared him acting like he was about to push him into the water.

"You need to quit playing like that boy! That's a lot of water to be playing with. You den lost yo mind fo real doing some crazy ass shit like that!"

On the way back from the Falls, it seemed to have a stern effect on everybody. The ride was tensed and mute. Bud was observing everybody and he broke the silence.

"So what up Larry, what you thinking about? Look like you have something on your mind?"

"We know what we about to do when we get back?" Tone jumped in.

"That nigga ain't about to do shit but get high. That nigga in too deep. He can't get his self together."

"Fuck you talking to lil' nigga! I will pull this van over and beat the snot out yo ass lil' nigga! I'll buy you and sell you like yo mama had you pussy ass nigga!"

"Okay Larry, that's enough! We get the point!" Lamika said seeing where Larry was going.

"So what happen to you Larry? You were one of the best to play the game. I mean you were well respected, had plenty of money. How Larry? I don't understand how you got to this point in your life, but this ain't the Larry we used to look up to."

Bud said looking out the window with a tear in his eye.

"In '79 I was making more money than I could dream of in the coke and pimpin' business. Other pimps did not have shit on me. I ran with the best. I got off track and fell hard for my bottom bitch Diamond, she fuck my whole world up from day one."

"Who is Diamond?" Pete asked.

"She chose me, she was working for Day-Day."

"You talking about Day-Day that host all the player ball picnics?"

"Yea, anyway she was a bad ass white bitch. Nigga was paying top dollars for a shot of that pussy. Some catz was paying two grand sometimes. One summer me and her went to Vegas. She showed me how good her pussy was, it was like gold. Niggas was going crazy for her. I mean she had gotten to the point to where the tricks were waiting in lines on the street corner for a shot of that pussy. She was making so much money I took her off the streets. Other pimps were trying hard to get Diamond. She was a loyal woman to me. When she started running the house, she started snorting coke. She was the baddest white bitch I ever laid eyes on at that time. By her being around me so much, we started fucking like lovers. We became more passionate about each other. One thing led to the next, then I ended up snorting coke. Then she started smoking then I started smoking."

"Where she at Larry?" Trina asked.

"What's so crazy is her and her boyfriend moved to Cleveland from Dallas. She was young as hell. Her boyfriend at the time was a rookie cop. Day-Day knocked her off a few months after she moved up here. At the time he had to give 15% of his money he was making off Prospect Ave to Pedro. What's so crazy is that Pedro had the rookie cop in his pockets too. Me and Day-Day started to bump heads about Diamond. One day she said she was going shopping. I have not seen her since. The word at that present time was her boyfriend killed her and was trying to start an investigation and pin the murder on Day-Day, but her body was never found. When the heat started coming down on Day-Day people did not suspect me to have nothing to do with her coming up missing, because I was on the down fall so it took a lot of heat off me. With the help of the rookie cop squeezing Day-Day out his money, he still had that stroll and he still was paying a percentage of his money if not more."

Larry and his generation paved the way for every generation after him. He had a concerned look of nostalgia on his face. After Larry told a little history about his downfall in life, it seemed like it put everybody into deep thought.

Bud had his mind already made up; he was cool on selling dope. He had a plug on the weed and on top of that, he was getting ready to start Barber College. The trip was right on time he was about to sit back and finally think about what direction he was headed in in life.

PW was taking it kind of hard after listening to Larry.

Damn maybe I should not be so hard on him like that, he been through a lot, just listening made PW realize that life can change for the better or for the worse at the drop of a dime. *If I don't do nothing I have to stay true and real to myself and no matter what I can't let no female take me off my shit,* PW continued to think himself.

Tone was so confused. His thoughts were all over the place. He knew they were getting money, he also knew he could beat Big Mike product and prices. His only reason for coming on this trip was to let them know he could beat the price they were paying for their product. Pete was the only person that was making him hesitant. His aggressiveness made him skeptical about showing his hand.

The only thing that was on Pete's mind was turning his hundred grand into a million dollars. It was not about the cars, or the clothes or even the women. All he wanted and cared about was money. Pete had been paying extra attention to Tone. He knew it was more to him. He couldn't pinpoint what it was. He made a mental note to do his homework on Tone.

While going through the PA turnpike Larry face was soaking wet with tears of failure. He made his mind up he was determined to get his life back on track. His main focus was to open up a car detailing shop. He wanted to show and prove to himself first then to Bud, he was the only person. He treated him the same and never looked down on him.

Chapter Six

Bud and Trina's birthday fell on a warm Sunday in September. PW pulled up hurting em. He redid the drop. The exterior was a candy root beer with a gold base ball with metallic flakes. What took the cake he had a clear plastic top. The interior was nasty. The inside was fiberglass. The dashboard was digital. The Lexani Strut grill had his initial inside the grill. The Lexani rims matched his Strut grill. The grooves of his rims were painted the same color as the car. His door handles were twenty four carat.

Meanwhile ...

Nutt had called Pete and informed him about a big time drug dealer from up the way named Ox, who was damn near supplying the whole city. They were on an eight hour stake out in a gated community in a small suburbs out in Avon Lake, which was on the outskirts of Cleveland.

"So who is this nigga Nutt?"

"I happened to be fucking with this chick the other day in Morris Black projects when Ox pulled up to holla at her older brother. The nigga getting money. He pulled up in that new joint, a S550 V12 all-white with the white rims kitted out and everything. Nigga hopped out like a ball player. He had on so much ice. Shit looked crazy. Ain't too many catz getting money like that in the City. I started playing the dumb roll. The more ole girl talked the more I learned about him. The nigga just opened up a club somewhere up Harvard Avenue. Come to find out, yo sister fucking with his lil' man."

"Who sister?"

"Yo sister nigga! Ole girl said he put Tone on about a year ago."

"Tone?" Pete asked in a high pitched voice.

"That bitch ass nigga. I knew it was something about that nigga man!"

"I don't know, but whatever happens we can't fuck this lick up bruh. They say slim worth a few tickets. Speaking of the devil, there go yo boy right there." Ox was backing out the three car garage when Nutt recognized the luxury sedan.

Bud was getting Trina's mother an ice cold pop out the cooler when his phone rang. It was the driver of the tow truck.

"Don't trip bruh; come all the way down to the yellow and white house."

When Bud pulled the car cover off his ole school, it was hard for some of the haters to understand the movement going on around them. His slab was the most anticipated slab of the summer. His '71 Cutlass was painted a Cadillac Escalade white, with a candy blue stripe around the muscle of the car. It was sitting on some offset rims. Twenty fours on the back and twenty-twos on the front.

The guts were all-white camel skin seats piped out in blue around the seats. The top of his car was all glass. The hood scoops added to the muscle of his car. Under the hood looked like a chrome factory. To take the cake he had Game God on his license plates. Big Mike was watching from the driveway. When everybody started to crowd around Bud's car.

I remember when that lil' nigga was born, Mike thought to himself. Mike was proud of Bud and how he carried it in the streets. You never seen him on the corner or spending his money on foolish things. He was doing better than some of the catz he started hustling with. Looking around and seeing everybody having a good time he noticed Pete was the only one missing. Before he could finish his thoughts Pete and Nutt pulled up in his two door Yukon dressed in all black. Before Pete could get out the truck, Peaches ran up on the truck.

"You had us on hold fo this nigga. I been calling your phone all day. You can't ever be on time for shit!" Pointing her index finger in his face.

"Fuck you talking about?" I do me I had some business to handle. Get the fuck out my face with that bullshit!"

"Or what Pete!"

He hit Peaches with a quick back hand forcing her to stumble back a few steps. It happened so quick she could not believe he hit her.

"I'm about to hurt you bitch ass nigga! You just hit me like that!" she said swinging on Pete. She was reaching in her pocket for her razor when Trina and Big Mike stepped in between the two.

"Take her in the house!" Mike said.

"Fuck you hit that girl fo, in front of all these people like that? You not only making yourself look bad, but you also making us look bad too!"

"How the fuck I'm making y'all look bad?" Fuck you talking about! Let me do me!" he said walking off.

"Y'all lil' girls got a lot to learn. Let them boys talk to you any kind of way, put they hands on y'all. They have no respect for a woman no more!"

Peaches were still crying.

"I remember one day Big Mike's father hit me. I waited until his black ass went to sleep and went up side his head with that all purpose black skillet. Hit his ass about three times before he woke up. His ass ain't hit me no more!"

PW walked in on the middle of their conversation. Giving her a hug.

Lamika walked in the kitchen to wash the barbeque sauce off her hands. She was blind to the fact that her brother just put hands to Peaches.

"Take her upstairs and clean her up." Granny D said shaking her head, while taking the three level lemon cake out the oven.

After everybody had left Granny D called Bud to her room.

"You listen to me don't never let me hear you putting your hands on a women. That's what cowards do when they cannot think outside their emotions. You have a good girl. You do right by her all that sleeping around ain't worth it. Think with your big head not your lil' head. Cover that thing up. I want to give you something. Your grandfather gave me this ring thirty five years ago, when we came up here from Alabama."

Club Mirage was in full fledge when the future stars walked and pulled up to the parking lot by the entrance. The line was wrapped around the corner. PW started picking women that was in line waiting. He picked out six dime pieces out the line to kick it with them.

Inside the club was jam packed. They went straight to the bar outside on the back deck.

"Happy B day my nigga" Pete said giving one of the females an unopened Moet bottle.

"Damn bruh I almost forgot to tell you happy B day my damn self!" PW said giving Bud a hug. The three comrades was looking out into the water, enjoying the view of the south bank area.

"On some real shit, y'all the only family I have. Man, life been so real after my mother and sisters got killed. It took all the love out my heart, but no matter what I went through y'all two niggas have always been the same and treated me like fam. I never told y'all but today is my two dead sisters' B day too!" he said throwing the empty Moet bottle in the lake.

"We here fo you bruh always!" Bud said putting his hand on his shoulders.

"I been thinking a lot bruh. Look Bud, you don't need to sell dope. Let me and PW handle that shit. You push that weed. It's time to tighten our circle up and keep it simple and basic, no extra shit. We gone stack our money and invest it into something that will pay off in the long run."

"See you been thinking bruh so what you want out of life?" Bud asked inhaling the weed.

"I don't know, I never looked at life like that. Long as my fam is happy I'm good. I hustle and live to put a smile on my family faces. I live for the moment, I'm not talented like y'all two niggas. I'm just good at getting money and hitting licks. The other day I got so high I started thinking extra hard. Sometimes I wonder will my greed be the death of me or force me to an early grave."

"Man why you hit Peaches like that earlier?"

"Man I don't know what the fuck has gotten into me lately, but I been so uptight just trying to get this money."

"Can't let the money dictate your actions bruh."

The three hustlers fell silent for a second listening to the nature of the waves hitting the foundation of the club.

"Fuck y'all so quiet fo? Hope y'all niggas ain't about to start that crying shit. Matter fact one of y'all roll up. Got these fine ass women around us. Shit I'm bout to do me." PW said pulling one of the females closer to him.

"Next year we docking the boat up to this bitch. V12 everything. Y'all know who has been MIA, that nigga Larry. I have not seen him in a few months." Bud said pulling the lighter from his linen shorts.

"That nigga was fly as hell when he stepped off that elevator. Could not tell him nothing that night." PW said laughing, spilling some of the Moet on his all-white Polo shirt.

"I respect that old ass nigga to the fullest. He has showed us a lot in these last past months. Larry is a good dude man." Pete said expressing his love for Larry.

Trina was flicking through the channels on the television when Bud walked through the door.

"Girl you still up?" Bud said taking his shirt off.

"Yea I was just up thinking."

"Bout what?"

"You know life and this baby and how little this apartment is for all three of us."

"Just one more year. That will give me enough time to save some extra money for a place out the way. Just relax I got you ma."

"You don't be scared leaving out the house knowing it is a possibility that you may never come back home."

"I don't think like that. Everything is in God's hands. Whatever happens is just meant to happen. I will never put myself in a situation to where I would leave you again. Last time you know what happened. Look I know how you feel and I understand that you have emotions and I will never play on those emotions. Let my role as a father and a man speak through my actions." He said putting his ears to her beach ball stomach.

Chapter Seven

NEW YEARS

"Push the head is coming out! Push Trina!" She had pushed out a five pound eight ounce healthy baby boy. Bud damn near passed out looking at Trina bring his son into this world of sin. He threw up twice while inside the delivery room. The first time was when his son whole body came out. The second time was seeing the sack of after birth. It was too much for him to stomach. After looking at Trina give birth he could not believe he put his mouth down there. It would be hard for her to get him to go downtown after what he just saw.

Tone had been calling Ox all day long. *Fuck up with this nigga,* he thought to himself. He finally picked up. "Young Tone, what up lil' nigga?"

"I been calling you all day."

"I know, I been ripping and running trying to make sure I have everything situated for tonight's New Year's party. Hate to run out of liquor you know how the New Year's crowd can get."

"I got this money fo you bruh."

"Listen … Listen just relax that money ain't going nowhere. No need to be in a rush bruh. Come out to the club and enjoy yourself. Take your mind off the streets for one night."

Ox took over club Starr Wars when Burt lost three hundred thousand dollars shooting dice a few weeks back. Two hundred thousand of the money was Ox's. With no cash to pay for his debt, he was forced to hand over the club or hand over his life. Ox had a strong hit man team that enforced their will on catz who decided to run off with money or felt like they could take all day to pay what they owed. Club Starr Wars perimeter was hedonism to anybody the scene was Robb Report inspired. Two parking lots one parking lot charged fifty dollars. You got two free drinks and two free pictures. The other parking lot was strictly for the heavy hitters. All the vehicles that was valet were by some of the finest women you could lay eyes on. They were dressed in a one piece leather cat suit. Once the cars were taking to the lot they would get VIP treatment. Full detail inside and out. The only way you could park in this lot is if you had a table reserved. The tables went from five hundred and up. Tone walked through the thick line dressed in a Sartorial silk-lined cashmere top coat, with a mink lapel and a detachable mink lining. A two bottom notch lapel cashmere, silk plaid blazer with a superfine double thread cotton shirt and a seven fold silk necktie with some Gucci frames on. The cologne by Gucci had him smelling like he looked.

Tone took pride in dressing in some of the most expensive designer clothes from all different designers in the US and overseas. Most of his clothes came from Italy.

Walking through the thick New Year's crowd inside the club, Tone made his way through the bulletproof glass doors to the VIP section of the club. Walking past a few ball players table and rap stars, he found Ox in the all-white section in the back of the room. All the tables in the all-white section were going for three grand.

Tone was greeted with genuine love from Ox and his family. This was his first time being introduced to a lot of people. He met a few drug lords from out of state. It was one well-groomed individual who was well put together. He was puffing on an expensive cigar. He had a hard time speaking English. He had two bodyguards standing behind him. He was dressed like an old mob boss, sitting with his legs crossed. His chair was positioned next to Ox's chair.

Ox felt like he owed Tone because his older brother took a fed case for him twelve years ago. They gave C-Lo fifteen years for five keys of cocaine. C-Lo was Ox's right hand man. They started of stealing cars together. Ox repaid his loyalty with opening the door for Tone to be able
to hold down the family financially and keep control over all his older brother's blocks.

"What's good young Tone, glad you could make it? Look around you, this is what it look like and feel like to hang out with money. You just in time. Grab you a few of them bottles and enjoy yourself."

Pete, PW, and Lamika brought New Year's to Trina's hospital room. They paid the cop at the desk two hundred bucks to let them in.

"Turn the music up Pete."

Ty was wired up to get a control buy off Deon from 59th in Fleet on the south side of town. Ty had sold his soul to the devil. Deon controlled his community with an iron fist.

Deon and his family had moved from Chicago when he was twelve years old. His father was a chief vice lord when he was younger. He showed Deon the foundation on how to build a strong street organization and the importance of structure inside his organization. Do to the help of his father, he had put together a ten man heroine operation. The FEDs started the investigation six months ago and could not get a phone conversation or a controlled buy.

His team was to discipline in their movements. The customers were too loyal. The product was coming from Africa. He set up shop on the south side of town in the sixth district. The neighborhood was dominantly white. The whole community as a whole did not fit in with the city's setting. It had more of a small hick town layout because of how poor the community looked. His spot was doing fifty to sixty grand a day. On Sundays at 5:00am, he would give away free dime bags just to show his appreciation to his customers. Sometimes the line would be two blocks long.

TY was the only person who could get close enough to him, because of the relationship he had with his older sister. TY pulled into Burger Spot. Deon was parked in an all-black Excursion truck, behind an all blue dumpster. He had state of the art technology inside his truck. The whole truck was bulletproof and surveillance all around the truck. Deon was in the last row of seats. He had a red bone driving and one gun which was sitting in the middle row.

TY opened the truck door to get in.

"Slow yo role playboy. Get in the passenger seat." The gunman said with his glock sitting on his lap. When TY hopped in the passenger's seat he was in a state of shock to find himself face to face with himself on the 25" monitor. His heart started to beat faster and his hands started to sweat. He felt defeated out the gate.

Officer Dixons was impressed at how Deon ran his operation. This was the closest they have gotten to the inside of his circle in the entire six months of their investigation. Officer Dixons was able to observe the inside of his truck with the help of the hidden camera inside his white gold godly piece.

The redbone turned the radio up from the steering wheel when Deon started to talk.

"Happy New Year's stranger. My sister was just talking about you last week at our Christmas dinner. My mother still got them earrings you gave her a few years back."

"Yea bruh you have a good family. How they been holding up over the years?" he asked as his face started to fill up with guilt.

"They been doing alright. My sister just had a lil' son four months ago. But other than that everybody cool. I know you came to talk business but unfortunately you gone have to wait until next year Joe." He said using Chicago streets slang.

Deon was five steps ahead of the game. He was typing what to say to his gun from the lab to that they had on their laps. TY could not turn around so he thought it was Deon talking over the music the whole time.

TY got caught with a 9mm handgun soon as the FEDs started picking up all gun cases. He would have ended up with a mandatory five years in the federal courts. With his background, it took him up three levels to a level 32 category five, a mandatory ten years, four years ago. By him being a CI the FEDs did not want his cover to get blown. Most of his jobs were done in other cities and states.

Officer Dixon and Hill was the two head federal agents working Deon's case. TY pulled up and met the two agents in Cleveland. Officer Hill was pacing back and forth with his hand folded across his chest. His head once filled with blond hair was now starting to thin out from the stress over the years as a federal agent. He had lost his wife and was on the verge of being kicked off the force.

Officer Dixon was a rookie agent. This was his first investigation. He was only twenty five years old young and a young black kid from upstate New York.

He blended in with any crowd. He was lean and in good health. He resembled the basketball star for the Heat Dwayne Wade.

Before TY could park his car officer Hill was opening the door for him.

"Damn can I park the car? Fuck you been drinking!"

"Look! I don't have time for the games. Either you get this kid to trust you enough to start doing business with you or your ass is out buddy!" he said pointing his finger in TY's face.

He walked up on Ty looking him in the eyes. Ty returned the stare. He blew the smoke from his cigar in Ty's face.

"I never said I could get you Deon. I said I can help. On top of that it's New Years. You two seen all that technology inside that truck. He three steps ahead of the game. Only way you can get close to him, you have to find the weakest link inside his circle. Anyway who does business on New Year's? I see why they about to get rid of yo drunk ass!"

Officer Hill hit Ty with two jabs to the stomach quick.

"You better watch your mouth you rat bastard! It's because of rat bitches like you that makes our job easy!"

Officer Dixon jumped in between the two. It was too late. Ty swung a mean wild right hook at Officer Hill, but the hit landed on the chin of Officer Dixon sending him to the pavement.

Officer Hill was in a state of shock looking at his rookie partner knocked out on the ground.

"Mutherfucker! I'm gone kill you for hitting my partner like that!" he said looking at officer Dixon, then back at Ty reaching for his gun.

Five Four Three Two One ... Happy New Year's! Club Star Wars was intensified by the time the ball dropped.

"Let's make a toast!" Ox said holding his glass in the air and his left arm around Tone. He could smell the liquor coming off Ox's breath.

"Toast to the Game God fo blessing us with all these fine ass hoes and all this money."

He took a seat on the all-white leather couch on the back wall of the VIP room. It was a flat screen plasma TV built into the wall showing Belly.

"I keep my ears to the streets. Heard you got yo foot in the door across town. That's a rough environment. Them boys down that way play fo keeps. It always been about the big takeout for them since back in the day.

"I know it always feel like I'm out of place when I'm down there. I guess because I'm out of my comfort zone. They some cool ass niggas doe. Just one is straight live wire, other than that they get money niggas. We all speak the same language when it comes to this money. One thing I do know is that they plug, which is their uncle, in a minute he want have enough work to supply them. If they keep mashing the way they are in these past few weeks. I just don't know how to tell them that I got work and can cover their order."

"Just relax its New Year's. Take your mind off the streets for one night. I got to go to the bathroom. Make sure nobody don't put shit in these open bottles."

Taking his 9mm off safety before he left out of the VIP room. Ox walked out the bathroom to find himself face to face with one of the baddest redbones he have seen in a long time. Starr was dressed down in leather Gucci jacket with the matching leather pants and some all black Gucci pumps. If looks could kill, Ox would have been dead five seconds ago. Seeing the lust in his eyes she moved in for the kill.

"You see something you like or something you can afford?" she said rubbing her index finger up the zipper of his all-white Prada jeans. Getting his lil' mans full attention.

"I never been the one to window shop ma. You know what they say all pussy ain't good pussy." he said rubbing his hands together looking at her ass.

"That's what I'm trying to tell you daddy. Some pussy come with a price. It's all about what you are willing to pay up to see how good this pussy really is."

Stepping closer to Ox wrapping her arms around his 5' 11" frame. Sucking on his bottom lip, she slipped her number inside his back pocket. She had planted the seed, all she had to do was give it some time and let it blossom overnight.

"Damn nigga! I thought you pissed on yourself. I was just about to come look fo you bruh."

"Man I just ran into a bad ass red bone. Bitch was strapped thick as shit."

"You better watch them hoes! All pussy ain't good fo you bruh. With the kind of money you making, every nigga in the city trying to get a piece of that bread."

"Fuck you doing?"

"I'm looking for my strap."

"Nigga you trippin'! You took your gun off safety before you went and used the bathroom. I told you them hoes will fuck yo shit all the way up."

Starr was sitting inside her five series unloading the bullets from Ox's 9mm. She could tell from the ice around his neck he was getting some real money. If she did not play her cards right she knew it was a good chance she could lose her life. Only thing that bothered her was the young cat that was in the VIP room with Ox. She could not put a name with his face.

The whole unit was drunk. C-Lo was fucking the Captain's wife, so he was able to control the compound and keep it flooded with contraband.

"This nigga must don't know why they call me C-Lo." he said blowing the dice. Bet fifty more meats on the six, eight."

Mckean medium was wide open. He had three more months left until he was eligible for the drug program. It would take eighteen months off his sentence and make him eligible for the halfway house.

It was a line of heads waiting to be experimented on when Bud walked through the door of the Barber College. Cutting hair came natural to him. By the time lunch came he had already cut ten heads.

It was a few individual he was cool with in the class, but he really didn't dialogue with them. He had one thing on his mind, getting his master license so he could open up his own barber college.

Trina and Lamika pulled up inside Beachwood Mall parking lot and went straight to the Gap store. They had been advertising the sell they had going on all week on the radio.

"Girl these lil' kids' clothes cost more than some of our clothes."

"Girl tell me about it."

"I'm glad I don't have kids!"

"Yet!" Trina said putting the jeans back on the clearance rack. After walking around and shopping they worked up an appetite. They ordered from the Best Steak restaurant inside the food court section.

"Slow down! Ain't nobody going to ask you for any of your food. You act like you have not eaten in five days!"

"When you called I was just waking up. I did not have enough time to fix me something to eat. By the time I got out the shower you were blowing the horn. Anyway how's life with a child?" Mika asked stuffing some cheese and bacon fries in her mouth.

"Its cool just can't get no dick or no sleep until lil' Bud goes to sleep. Most of the time his father have him. That nigga been acting like super dad. He so over protective about his son."

"You better be glad he is a good father. You don't want for nothing. He keep money in your pocket, the house is plushed out and you have a nice car. On top of that you getting good in house dick. I hope my brother do something with his self. Ever since we came up here from Alabama after our oldest brother got killed, it did something to our family. Shortly after that mom dukes went downhill."

"Granny D, Bud and Big Mike the only family we have. It's hard trying to be cool with fake ass people out here. Pete crazy ass don't want nobody coming over the house. He get mad when Tone come over. Tone ole scary ass be acting like he scared of Pete lil' ass!" They grabbed their bags walking towards the exit.

"Damn excuse you!" Lamika said to the dude who just bumped into her.

"Say what lil' ma!" When Lamika turned around she was face to face with Ty.

"Girl what the hell you doing out here with yo thick ass?"

"Boy you almost got slapped!"

"Anyway! I see you shopping good. Must be nice to have somebody to spoil you like that. See y'all got a lot of bags. You and your friend!"

"She ain't a friend she family. That's Bud's baby mother." Trina was not feeling the vibe she was getting from Ty.

"Look Ty, we about to leave. If you don't mind, give me your number and I'll hit you up."

On their way back Trina could not wait to ask Lamika about Ty and how she knew him.

"Who was that dude back there you was talking to?" Trina asked changing lanes on the freeway.

"Girl Ty, he grew up with us. He just moved to the west side of Cleveland a few years back. He stayed in the white house on 83rd street behind Granny D's house for years before they moved."

"Something about him I don't like."

"Girl Ty ain't gone hurt nobody. We always had a crush on each other when we were younger."

"You better watch yourself with that nigga." Trina's phone started ringing.

"Hello?"

"What up, where you at?" a nosey Bud asked.

"You got my son with you?"

"Damn let me answer the first question you asked before you ask another question. I'm leaving the mall me and Lamika. Your son is over my mother's house."

"Look do me a favor. Pick my food up from Calypso's and I will pick BJ up from your mother house."

"Come on Big Mike this us. You act like we ain't good for it. We putting in work around here. Get me and Pete together for this sixty stacks."

"Y'all lil' nigga think y'all slick. I ain't gone always be here fo y'all when y'all come short. Y'all don't come short with them other niggas when y'all trying to get right. This the last time I'm gone do this fo y'all lil' nigga. Where y'all money at?"

"See that's the problem we need you to front it to us." Pete said.

"Nigga what?! Front what?! You niggas den lost y'all mind!"

"See we was just fucking with you tight ass nigga!" PW said throwing him six ten thousand dollar stacks.

"Y'all lil' nigga need to quit playing so much."

"We want our shit soft too, with yo slick ass!" Pete said fixing his Polo jeans.

"Tone what's good? You in the hood?"

"Yea why, what's up?"

"I got a play for you. Meet Ace inside the gas station on Harvard. He got three stacks fo you.

"Ox why you always calling my phone with that hot shit. I told you about that. You never know who listening to these phone calls!"

"Nigga quit crying. Make sure you handle that. Don't never say I never gave you nothing." Ox said looking in his rearview mirror.

"Where you at? Why you can't meet him?"

"I'm out the way, bout to go out to eat."

"You tricking already. Who you got ole girl from the New Year's jump off with you?"

"Yea you know me." He said grabbing the back of Starr's head. Her relentless head game was mean, forcing Ox to veer off into the middle lane on the freeway. Starr was good at playing her role to get what she wanted. If it was not for Pete she would still be living in the project with her smoked out prostitute mother. He put her through cosmetology classes and helped her get her own crib and car. It was all business with her.

Pulling up to Red Lobster. Starr was cleaning Ox's limp penis with a baby wipe.

"Welcome to Red Lobster. May I take your order?" The young college student asked.

"Yea let me get two shots of Grey Goose straight. And whatever she wants John." Ox said looking at the waiter's name tag.

"Let me get a glass of apple juice until I find what I want to order." Starr did not smoke or drink. She worked out three times a week keeping her frame tight.

"We will be ready to order when you come back." She said looking at the menu.

"So Starr tell me something about you?"

"What you want to know?" She looked him in the eyes to let him know he had all of her attention. They were sitting in a nonsmoking section off to the back of the restaurant.

"Here's your drinks. You two ready?"

"Let me get a shrimp platter." Ox ordered.

"Let me get the chicken and shrimp Alfredo with garlic bread."

"Ox I will be right back." Ox could not keep his eyes off her back side. Something about her had him open.

Deon phone rang several times. He still did not pick up. Officer Dixon was getting fed up with Deon street smarts. It seemed like he was always two or three steps ahead of them. Officer Hill was under a lot of stress lately. His wife and the force were bringing heat down on him. A few months back before Officer Dixon joined the force him and a few other agents were involved in a few houses getting raided. They were using their CI to get tips on drug dealers who were selling kilos of dope. They had a four man team within the force. Officer Hill Cuban informant gave him information about the wrong drug lord. When the four officers entered the house it was an old Cuban lady in her late 60's sitting in a luxury recliner leather chair when the agents kicked in the door in. Laying her on the ground. They rampaged the house, coming away with 50 kilos of pure heroin and two million dollars in cash. The money was stashed in the floor underneath the chair the old lady was sitting in. The drugs happened to belong to the younger brother of the Santana drug cartel from Miami.

Little did the force know, Officer Hill was supplying the product to an African who he didn't know was the main supplier and source for young Deon, which they have under investigation.

The reality of his actions hit him dead smack in the face a week after the product hit the streets. The cartel visited Officer Hill at his house one morning before going to work with a picture of his kids playing at school. If he did not pay all the money back and, the drugs he and his family was dead.

The day they were called into Bank's office he then realized his freedom was on the line as well. The heroine that was dropped inside the teacher's bathroom was actually from his product. Putting two and two together. The African he was selling the heroine to was the one supplying it to Deon. Now his main focus was trying to get his rookie partner to feed into his plan on robbing drug dealers for their money and products.

"I don't know what to tell y'all he might call back then again he might not. Just be patient."

"Don't put too much soda on it nigga!" Pete said to PW.

"I got this nigga! I was taught by the best. Been doing this shit here when you was pissing in the bed my nigga. Sit back and watch magic!"

Pete could hear his cell phone ringing in the other room on the charger. Seeing it was Starr he picked up.

"What up ma. How that business going?"

"Everything 100 got this nigga wide open. I got some homework for you. The name and the face look so familiar to me, but I cannot put it together. His name is

Tone. I saw him at the New Year's party, just can't put a face with the name or where I know him from."

"Don't even trip off that. I got you on that end. Just be safe ma one!" Starr brushed her teeth and left out the bathroom.

Deon called back. Officer Dixon answered the phone.

"Hello somebody called my phone?"

"Hold on this is not my phone, its Ty phone!"

"You got other nigga answering your phone and shit. What type of time you on Joe?" Using his Chi town street slang.

"Naw bruh it ain't even like that. I was in the other room. What the deal doe? I'm trying to get right."

"You trying to get right huh? You still pumping on the west side?"

"Shit been going, I can't complain. They just looking for a better choice of drug. You the only one who can make it happen from what I hear in the streets. I been moving around a lil' bit, I found it to be real beneficial to both of us. I been going hard on W 14th in Clark all the way down to Storer Avenue."

"Sounds good bruh. You know me bruh. It's all business. Since I fuck with you. I'll meet you inside the bathroom at KFC on 55th in Broadway."

"Told y'all he was going to call back." Officer Hill had other intentions. He needed to make sure his thought was correct. Once he got the ounce he was going to get it tested to make sure it was the same heroine that he has been supplying his African mans with.

"Ty all we need is an ounce, to get this ball rolling." Officer Hill gave Ty three grand and hid the camera inside his top button on his Polo shirt.

By the time Trina made it home, Bud was in the bathroom washing his son up.

"I'm glad you started getting him ready for bed." Trina said sitting the bags down next to the chocolate leather couch.

She walked in the bathroom. He washed BJ's hair.

"A Tee he got hair just like me don't he?"

"You think so?"

"So what you get at the mall? Look like you spent every penny I gave you."

"Boy quit playing. You know females when we shop we can spend fifty dollars and make it look like we spent a lot. Here let me finish that your food is on the table by the door. Turn that music down, I got a headache. Hey mommy lil' man." She said splashing the warm water on his young body making him smile.

"Nigga I told you I was a beast in the kitchen. Brought you back an extra five hundred grams nigga. I'm trying to show you how to become a rich man. Hope you stacking that money. I will cook the rest of this shit tomorrow."

Ty been inside KFC for about 20 minutes, still no Deon. The two agents sat inside a beat up 1977 Chevy Caprice Classic. Rodney walked inside KFC dressed in all black with his hood on looking like he was about to stick the place up. He made eye contact with Ty. He beat Ty into the bathroom. Rodney was tying his shoe. Deon never did any hand to hand business.

"It's inside the last stall. Drop the money on the floor. He told me you was good peeps, so I threw in an extra three grams on the strength."

By the time Ty came from out of the stall Rodney was gone. Officer Dixon had taken pictures of everybody who parked inside the parking lot since they been there and wrote down all the license plates. He could not find anybody that came out of KFC with a hat and a hood on.

Rodney parked his truck inside that parking lot every day at the same time and left at the same time every day. He had a friendly relationship with Tasha who worked at the cash register. She was cool with Deon's sister. Once he left out the bathroom he took off his hat and hoodie and put the different fit on giving Tasha the money so she could take it to Deon's sister. It was a routine that would never get disrupted. Tying his shoe kept Ty from getting a look at his face. That's why he put the ounce inside the stall, so he would never be face to face. All they saw was a man with a hood and hat on when he walked passed their car again with different clothes on they paid him no mind. To take the cake, his truck was parked right next to their car. They were through off from the jump, because he caught the bus to meet. Ty was inside KFC. When Ty was coming out, Rodney was pulling off.

Tone called Lamika.
"What you doing?"
"I'm about to get in the shower."
"Do me a favor before you get in."
"What's that?"
"Unlock the door for me."
Tone pulled up to Lamika's apartment on the Blvd in less than ten minutes. He walked in to the sound of R. Kelly oscillating through the surround sound system. He walked into the bathroom to find Lamika with her back to the shower head letting the hot water run through her long natural hair. He watched her from the doorway idolizing her natural beauty. Her cocoa butter skin tone complimented her 36C breast and a 32" butt.

Tone started undressing. Lamika felt his presence. She began to massage her nipples, while sticking two of her fingers inside her juice box, while looking at Tone seductively. She took her two fingers from her juice box and began tasting them. Tone slid the glass shower door back and joined her.

Tone began to passionately kiss Lamika on the back of her neck. The steam from the hot water caused the bathroom to fog up. Tone rubbed his hard muscle between Lamika's soapy ass cheeks. He entered her wet pussy from the back. Feeling his warm penis penetrate her caused her to climax. She bit down on her bottom lip and let out a loud moan. Hitting her left wall made her moan even louder. Lamika contracted her pussy muscle. releasing everything he had inside of him. he was breathing extra hard and his legs was beginning to give out. Tone was holding on to Lamika with his mouth wide open with his chin pinned in the middle of her back. He still had his rod inside her juice box.

Chapter Eight

Ox pulled up to a newly constructed brick house with a three car garage. Two trained red nose pit bulls

---

"So how you like barber school?" Trina asked Bud.

"I mean it's worth it. At the end it will pay off. I look forward to it. Plus I might have to line the back of that nappy ass neck up."

"Oh! You got jokes!" Trina said as she playfully hit him with her son in her other arm.

Ox's garage was custom built. His living room and garage was connected. The dining room floor was 8" x 8" handmade concrete tiles infused with pewter and ivory colored pigments. The space also included an antique William IV Mahogany dining table from the 19th century. He also had French chandelier. A trio of Han Dynasty furniture complimented with an elegant coffered ceiling.

He turned the *Best of Al Green.*

"Make yourself at home."

Starr relaxed in the inside Ox's all-white Ralph Lauren TV room. Looking around she could tell white was her favorite color. Ox was her type. He was short, cocky and confident with a mean swag about himself. Ox's hand on her shoulder made her flinch. He wasn't wearing nothing but a Gucci robe. He still had water specks running down his back and chest.

"You ain't get bored did you?"

"Naw, I'm cool." She said as she turned around to face Ox's muscular physique. He led her to his master bedroom that was furnished with a black Chinois Erie four poster, an 18th Century European limestone fireplace and a marble patio with a sitting area that led to his bedroom. He also had water fixtures that turned into a waterfall that spilled into his swimming pool.

The windows in his bathroom gave off natural light. His bathroom had heated marble floors when the temperature was below 20 degrees outside. The bathtub was a terra-cotta colored marble the matched the floor. A 19th Century Alabaster chandelier and an English Chinois Erie table also decorated the space with two separate dressing rooms with his and her walk-in closets.

Ox kissed Starr on the neck softly, followed with another kiss hitting her spot. She couldn't resist. His aggressiveness was turning her on even more.

Starr was rubbing her finger through his ripped midsection. Ox laid her naked back against the cashmere and mink blanket. She could feel his penis maturing through the robe. By the time Ox finished undressing Starr, she was wet as a pool.

He couldn't believe how flawless her body was. She didn't have a stretch mark or a scar. She looked even better naked. He slid his tongue in her ass. In the bedroom Ox was a freak. She was grabbing the back of his head while his tongue was in motion.

Ox tried to enter her raw. She made him stop and get a condom. Once he penetrated her walls, he could feel the heat and the wetness from her inside taking control of his penis. He had to check and make sure the condom didn't bust. Starr straddled him and was riding him from the back making each ass cheek bounce one at a time. Ox's legs began to shake and his toes locked up from the pressure Starr was applying. She jumped off Ox taking the condom off before he was about to climax. Ox thought she was a porn star. His toes curled as she swallowed the majority of his future kids. Ox was stretched out breathing hard across his ten thousand dollar bed.

When Ox picked up his ringing phone it was 10:4am.

"Nigga I been calling you all morning. Fuck you doing, you gone sleep the day away!"

"I'ma call you when I'm coming down the street."

He dozed off for about five minutes. Starr had his limp penis in her mouth. She was gagging from the length and size of his rod hitting the back of her throat.

Starr gripped the bottom of his rod. Within seconds she was on top of him grinding her hips. Ox was not in control Starr felt his body getting weak.

"Good morning daddy." Starr said with Ox's penis still pinned up in her guts. Ox was watching the young tender's ass bounce back and forth into the bathroom. She came back out with a soapy rag to clean him up. By the time he got out of bed Tone was on the intercom at the gate, he saw his car on the monitor, he let him in.

Tone was the only person he let come to the house and do business. The house Pete and young Nutt was casing out was his mother's place. Starr was in the shower when Tone walked through the door.

"What's good big bruh? Man you been in bed all morning, that ain't like you bruh."

Starr heard a familiar voice she peeked over the third floor balcony. She could see the face of the young cat who was in the VIP room with Ox on New Year's. She couldn't remember where she seen his face before.

"It just was a long night bruh."

"So what you gone fuck the day away."

"Pussy makes the world go round; you should try some one day." Ox said pouring a glass of orange juice.

"I got that 60 grand fo those three bricks you fronted me and I got 80 of my own money. Oh! I knew it was something I wanted to ask you. When was the last time you talked to my brother?"

"I talked to him last week after I met with dat lil' white broad to give him that weed he had asked for. I just put a grand on his account the other day, he told me you and your mother was supposed to come and see em and send him some horizon magazines."

"My moms might go see em this weekend coming up. I might go. He walked that shit down. It seem like that nigga been in jail fo eva."

"Yea my nigga short now." He said grabbing the duffle bag off the floor.

"Be right back."

Tone turned the flat screen on inside the kitchen to ESPN. Hearing Ox coming up the steps Star ran back into the bedroom. He entered the bedroom. Starr was standing in the mirror oiling up. Ox walked inside his walk in closet. He hit the switch that led to a trap door inside his personal closet. Not paying Starr any attention. She could see everything he was doing from the angle she was positioned in the mirror. Ox put eight bricks inside the duffle bag and placed the money inside an alloyed safe he had built into the floor.

While he was sleep Starr cased his house from top to bottom. She found both spots where he kept his guns and also stumbled into his monitor room he had in the basement. She unloaded all his guns.

Ox came back downstairs with eight bricks for Tone. He was eating a peanut butter and jelly sandwich on wheat bread.

"Be safe my nigga." Ox said while handing Tone the duffle bag full of bricks leaving Ox in deep thought.

Tone walked out the door finishing his sandwich. Tone and his brother was some loyal niggas at heart. C-Lo was just a tad more aggressive than Tone when he was Tone's age. From phone conversation and visits. Ox could tell time had matured his closest childhood friend over the twelve years he been down.

Ox had a relationship with his connect if something was to happen to him before C-Lo came home; He knew to keep things pumping with Tone until C-Lo came home.

The night of Ox's New Year's party he was sitting next to mogul Santana, one of the biggest drug cartel in the MIA. He was no stranger to Cleveland. Fifteen years ago the Santana brothers came to Cleveland for the first time to settle some unfinished business.

Chapter Nine

Peaches entered the door of Lamika's apartment. She was greeted to the smell of sautéed onions, hamburgers and French fries.

"Pete been calling here every five minutes looking for you, acting all crazy and shit. I hope you ain't pussy whip my brother!" She said removing a batch of French fries from the skillet.

"I ain't thinking about your crazy ass brother! My phone went dead. On top of that, I got the biggest headache. I need to take a shower."

Twenty minutes later Pete walked through the door. He grabbed some fries off the stove with his dirty ass hands.

"Bout time yo lazy ass cooked. Did Peaches call yet?"

"Naw I haven't heard from her."

Pete entered his room closing the door behind him, Peaches was standing behind him with a towel wrapped around her. She jumped on Pete's back forcing him to the bed. He reached for his .22 rifle His street instinct kicked in. Hearing Peaches giggling made him laxed.

"Girl you better stop playing so much. I probably would of shot yo ass if I could got to my gun."

"Nigga you wouldn't gone do shit! Look inside the closet I got something for you."

Pete looked in the closet.

"What I'm looking fo?"

"Move! Yo ass can't do shit right." Peaches pushing him to the side

"Where the hell you get this from?"

Pete had been looking for a Mack 10 .38 caliber for a few weeks. It shot 1,250 rounds per minute. Pete couldn't wait to put in some work.

"What's the deal with ole boy?" Pete asked observing his weapon of mass destruction.

"It's too early to tell. I'm just playing my role."

"Look! Don't fuck this up, stay focused. We both need this lick." Pete said walking to the closet.

"I need $200."

"That's all you need? You got that." Pete said reaching in his pocket peeling off $500 before walking out the room.

Chapter Ten

PW walked inside the Barber College taking a seat inside Bud's chair.

"Don't fuck my hairline up!" PW said.

"Nigga you got me fucked up! I ain't never fucked nobody's hairline up!" he said putting the black smock around PW's neck.

"Fuck you dressed like that for?"

"Like what?"

"Like you about to go on a job interview or something."

"This the dress code bruh either this or hit the streets."

"How you want this nappy shit?" Bud asked as he ran a comb through PW's hair.

"Cut a lil' bit off the top and taper the sides and back."

"So what's good?" Bud asked turning the clippers on.

"Shit!" Everything is everything. Just need a plug. Big Mike got his foot on our neck right now. I mean the product good, but god damn. You ain't been in the mix since your son been born. What's good with you bruh?"

"Yea bruh had to fall back for a second. You know with school then after school. Some nights I have to come here and get my hours. Don't get it twisted; I'm still on the grind. I'm just trying to do something with my money." He said turning PW around to blend the left side of his taper in.

"I feel you bruh. I wouldn't mind opening up a paint shop. I love ole school cars."

Bud spun him around in the chair again looking at his finished work. He was impressed.

Ty put his cell phone on speakerphone. He was driving down on the west side of Cleveland when Lamika rang his cell phone.

Hearing an unfamiliar female voice he asked, "Who dis?" while inhaling the blunt.

"So now you acting like you don't remember who you gave your number to huh?"

"What you want Lamika? What took you so long to call?"

"Ty I'm been calling you for the past few days."

"I'm out the way right now. Can I call you later at this number?"

"Don't forget either."

"Girl you always fucking with somebody man!" Peaches said flat ironing Lamika's hair in the kitchen.

"I been knowing Ty since back in the day. Me and Trina ran into him at the mall the other day."

"Whatever happen to ole boy you went out of town with you?"

"Tone, he was over here last night. I fucked him to sleep, why you ask?"

"I just ain't seen you with him in a while. Speaking of the devil what's up with Trina. I ain't seen her since she done had her son. Bud got her ass locked down."

"She been going to school. Trying to get her RN license. You might see her before you leave."

"God damn, who dat?" A voice floated through the air.

All the barbers were pop eyed when Shanell walked in with her four year old son Vernon. Bud so happen to have the only open chair.

"What's good? He spoke with confidence.

"I'm good. I need my son haircut. Something nice that will last for two weeks."

"I got something you might like." He said making a wooden 2" x 4" booster for the barber chair.

"Come on lil' man." Bud said picking her son up.

"What's your name?" Bud asked.

"Boy tell him yo name and quit acting like you shy!"

"My name Vernon." He said in a low pitched voice.

"You just started?"

"Yea a few months ago. You know something different that pays." Bud responded while sanitizing his clippers before using them.

"You don't mind me asking your name do you?" She asked.

"They call me Bud, that's cool with you?" He answered making eye contact.

Shanell could feel the chemistry. She was flawless. She had beautiful skin without a bump or a scar. She had long jet black hair, no weave and she was down to earth. She had nice legs, a flat stomach and a fat ass.

Bud put a clean bald fade on Vernon.

"Here you go lil' man." He said giving him a pack of grape *Now and Laters*, after dusting the dead hair off him.

"So if it's cool can I call you one of these days? washing his hands in the back bar.

"I can do that for you." She said observing her son's haircut. She put an extra pep in her step knowing all eyes were on her.

"Damn nigga! You always get lucky for some reason. You get all the heads to cut." Dre said cleaning his 76ers clippers.

Bud was trimming his goatee in the mirror.

"Sometimes it's just how the ball bounce my nigga."

Pete answered his cell phone. He was handing a smoker three bus downs for 50 dollars.

"What up? What we looking like, you ready to make that move?" PW was on the other line.

"I just got here. It's doing what it always do. Where you at?"

"I'm headed that way. I just left Bud getting a haircut. I'll be there in about ten minutes."

Pete responded to the knock on the front door.

"Who is it?" He asked grabbing his 357 off the table, before looking through the peephole of the tarnished wooden door. There was an unfamiliar face on the other side dressed in an old Cleveland Cavalier basketball jacket, with a pair of fitted stones washed jeans, He was in desperate need of a shave.

Pete opened the door with force, aiming the gun directly in the smoker's face.

"Hold on young blood, don't shoot me! I'm just trying to get me a bump fo this here forty dollars, so I can get right with this lil' tender I got." He said wiping the corner of his mouth as he pulled two crumbled twenty dollar bills from his filthy pocket of his jeans.

Pete placed two bus downs in his hand. An unmarked vehicle slowly parked in the background. Three police cars were in position for the undercover control buy.

PW parked on the next street over where he always parked and-walked through cut that led to the back door of the trap house. For some reason he left his car running.

PW entered through the unlocked back door.

"Pete!" he yelled out.

"Nigga why you got the back door unlocked like that for a nigga!"

Pete was making sure the front door was locked. When PW got to the front door he could hear the screeching tire from the police cars coming to a halt in front of the house.

"Po Po!" PW said running past Pete. *Boom* A big black street detective in street clothes kicked the wooded door in with one kick. The two hustlers sprinted toward the back door, hitting the fat overweight cop in the face with the door forcing blood to splash from his broken nose. They hit the cut full speed and hopped inside the Chrysler 300.

Eeeeeerrrrtttt The two tires were spinning in place before catching grip to the gravel. They were coming out on 82nd and Wade Park and two cop cars were in hot pursuit.

"Pete looked in the glove box and handed me that work!" He made a left hand turn on 88th and Wade Park coming through the alley, back up 84th making a left back onto Wade Park. It was just enough to shake the two cop cars that was accelerating towards the direction of 92nd Street.

Taking-them toward 92nd St. PW turned inside Daniel E. Morgan elementary school parking lot forcing the cars to slow down their pursuit due to the fact that school was letting out. PW could hear more police cars getting closer.

"Nigga drive this slow as car!" PW just missed a third grader swerving onto the sidewalk hitting the horn. He ran over a brown garbage can sending it 15 feet in the air.

"Move ... Move ... Move the hell out of the way!" He yelled waving his left arm out the window while driving on the local residents front lawns trying to elude law enforcement

"Look soon as I hit this left onto the mainline police gone be all over us. When we hit 87th Street we gone have to do what we do. Whatever happen I will meet you back on the Duce!"

Pete and PW retreated out the moving vehicle. Sending the automobile crashing into a wooden telephone pole.   .

"Two suspects are now on feet!" The police radioed. Pete cleared the six foot fence like a high jumper.

The oversized officer had one too many *Little Debbie's* he was out of breath within two minutes of the foot chase. PW never looked back. He took every cut that led him to Granny D's backyard. Lucky for Pete, Peaches' mother stayed on 89th and Ansel. He hid on her back porch.

Trina and her mother were having a mother to mother conversation

"How has you and Bud's relationship since you had BJ, has he changed or been acting funny. You know sometimes after they have a child with you they fill like you ain't going nowhere."

"Ma we are fine. Me and Bud relationship is getting stronger every day, no need for you to keep asking questions about what he represents as a man or a father."

"Honey I'm just trying to make sure you and your son are taken care of. I'm just worried about you." She said letting out a deep sigh.

"Ma you did a hell of a job molding me into this woman. I'm mature enough to make responsible decisions in life without you being around, I am sorry."

PW knocked on Granny D's back screen door, lightheaded trying to catch his breath. His heart was beating uncontrollably. Big Mike came to the door eating a fried ham and cheese sandwich. With salad dressing stuck inside the corner of his mouth.

"Nigga what the fuck wrong with you old boy!" Mike said while he used his tongue to suck the bread from in between his teeth.

"Hell you sweating like that for?" He asked taking another bite out of his sandwich.

"Main let me in I just was running for my life and you want to play games and shit!"

Mike stepped to the side to let PW in, looking at him up and down.

"You need to wipe yo mouth with yo phatt ass. Me and Pete was on a high speed chase!"

"Where he at?" He asked cutting PW off in mid-sentence.

"We split ways on 87th. That's the last time I seen him!"

"What happen?" Big Mike asked with an earnest facial expression.

"All I know is I called him when I was coming from getting my hair cut. Pulled up to the spot. I wasn't inside a good two minutes police ran up through the front door."

Big Mike phone rang. He could hear the sirens in the background as an out of breath Pete .spoke through the receiver. Big Mike pulled up to the stop sign on 89th and Ansel in a triple black 96SS Impala sitting on 24" LX-2 Lexani rims, with the strut grill to match. Two police cars flew past them as they were coming to a complete stop.

Pete wasn't in the car ten seconds before PW started grilling him.

"Who the hell you served?"

"I only hit two licks and one was some old head fo 40."

"He had to be an undercover. If I would have never came by yo ass would have been ass out."

"Y'all lil' niggas need to slow down!"

Chapter Eleven

Lamika had been calling Ty for the past two hours.

"Girl stop calling that nigga." Peaches said cleaning her hand bag out.

"He gone call back if he wants some pussy."

Tone and Ox was sitting on 145th Kinsman inside Ox's Range Rover observing the lower level street hustlers scramble back and forth, running up on customer's cars who pulled up to acquire about their choice of drug.

"Look Tone I want you to know something. I'm not just doing this for your brother sake. I'm doing this because you earned it. I'm thinking about falling back after my Birthday. I'm trying to go out on top. I'm up bruh. The club doing numbers. I got property out of state. I'm set for life. I've been watching how you handle yourself out here. I know you ready to step up. It would be selfish of me to hold you back. I'ma fall back so you can get you a nice run, then you can lock down the streets of Cleveland. When yo time comes don't buy nothing with your money that will draw attention. Fuck them cars. I'm not telling you not to floss or not to have fun, but do it out of town bruh. The man is more important than the money. Money is more important than the floss. Freedom is more important than it all. Keep yo circle tight. You should have at least three cell phones. Never let nobody call you from their everyday phone. Invest all your money into something that has value and can make you some money for the years to come."

Tone was inhaling all the game Ox was giving him. Ox's phone interrupted, it was Starr.

"What's good daddy? Long time no hear from."

"I'm good. I'm up the way right now, I'ma call you back in about 20 minutes."

"Don't forget."

"Nigga all that fucking I'm surprised yo ass ain't got no kids."

"Safe Sex is the best sex my nigga!"

Chapter Twelve

"You have five more minutes on your test." The barber instructor yelled out. Bud was proof reading his test before turning it in to Mr. White on his way out Mr. White delayed his movements.

"How you doing Mr. Davis? I have been paying close attention to you. I'm going to do you a favor. State board is coming up. I know what you are going to say, but relax I understand you do not have all the hours that's required but you have the skills. I'm going to make it happen for you. Don't let me down."

"I won't. Thanks Mr. White!" Bud said extending his right hand out to shake the instructor's hand.

"You two in my office now." Lieutenant Banks said slamming his office door behind him. Lieutenant Banks was fed up with the progress of the conspiracy case with Deon.

"Do you two have any solid evidence against this kid that can stick in the six circuit district of courts, other than pictures?"

"Well as of a few days ago we got our first control buy. This kid is not your average drug dealer for his age. I think he has an excellent IQ of criminal intelligence that separates him from the rest." Agent Dixon said.

"I don't give a damn how smart he is the heat is coming down on me hard. The head of DEA and Internal affairs are asking questions about this kid. I don't give a damn what happens I want this son of a bitch off my fucking streets!"

He said throwing the Cleveland Newspaper on the desk for the two agents could see what the fuss was about. The front page read: *Drugs starting to leak inside the Cleveland Public schools. A gram of grade a heroine was found inside the teacher cafeteria at South High school.*

"Either you two step your game up or I'm taking both of you off the case!"

"Agent Hill you got this rookie with you. You haven't showed him nothing." Lieutenant Banks said slamming his right fist onto the desk.

Big Mike, Pete and PW was sitting inside the Gentlemen's Club watching China slide down the pole head first reversing and flipping landing into a split then bouncing up and down to the chemistry she had with the music. *I'm in love With a Stripper by T-Pain* vibrated through the speakers.

China was topless. She was the most requested strippers in the Gentlemen's Club.

She had with the-music—that vibrated through the atmosphere. China was top less she's one of the most requested strippers in the club. This was Pete's first time inside a strip club.

PW was getting a lap dance from Co Co. She was a chocolate 24 year old with a blond quick weave. She was dancing to pay for her last year of medical school at Case Western College.

"Say lil' ma we can end all this playing house shit. I got three hundred fo some of dat pussy!" PW whispered in Co Co's ear. She grabbed PW's hand. He had pre cum all over the inside of his boxers.

Big Mike was pissy drunk hopping on stage with China. Pete was ready to rob all the strippers. They all was nasty hoochies to him.

Matt had been in court all day. He was looking at seven years in the state if convicted and if Ty came to court on him. Matt couldn't believe Ty would set him up. He was the one who showed him around the west when he moved on the west side. He should have listened to YG the night they was outside on the block.

"Matt that nigga had a gun on him the night the vice hit the strip he was the only one who got knock that night!"

As he walked out of the Justice Center in downtown Cleveland he blazed a cigarette. Letting his thoughts chase the wind. He knew what had to be done.

"PW hold that nigga up so I can get a picture of this shit. This shit is a classic!"

119

Pete and PW was in tears laughing at Big Mike. He had got so drunk he pissed on his self on the stage with China. Then had the nerve to pass out with his pants down.

"Man this nigga got the biggest shit stain I ever seen." Pete said taking a picture of Big Mike.

Officer Hill was parked outside his ten year old daughter school, when he received a call from one of his confidential informants. Informing him about a Haitian drug dealer that he was fifty grand in debt with. Jennifer opened the passenger's door of the all-black Crown Vic just as he was ending his conversation to make his illegal incursion on the Haitian operation.

Blending in with traffic, he asked his daughter how her day went. This was their daily routine before taking her to performance art practice. He realized he was being followed by an all-black GMC pickup truck with midnight tint on all the windows.

After dropping Jennifer off he was still was being tailed. Making a left hand turn off Highland Avenue onto a residential street. He pulled over to allow the driver of the truck to bypass him. When the truck did not proceed he started to tense up. The driver of the pickup truck overbearing the gas pedal gained momentum to bring the truck to a violent halt. From the back window of the truck a young gunman raised his AK-47 and smiled at Officer Hill.

Chapter Thirteen

Uptown was full of pedestrians going and coming on their 12:00 lunch break. Two internal affairs agents had set up surveillance inside an old room on the 2nd floor of the Ballers building. Across the street from the newly constructed condos on 18th Street. The room was filled with empty pizza boxes and pop bottles from their days of surveillance.

The agents were equip with the best technology the US government could provide for them. The lens on the tripod was inbounded with a zoom lens of 200 enabling the agents to see your sweat glands on your forehead. The night before they set up small speaker devices inside every room.

Officer Hill and Dixon pulled up in front of the condos in a white Direct TV van dressed as employees for the TV Company. They grabbed their tools from the back of the van.

"What the hell is going on in their? I'm getting a lot of movement through my headset." The agent said polluting the volume in his headset. The other agent was looking through the tripod. Zooming through the Haitian apartment trying to see what his partner was talking about. Seeing the Haitian stacking stacks on top of stacks of money into a tan duffle bag.

"May I help you two gentlemen?" The attractive blue eyed blond receptionist at the front desk asked.

"One of our customers has been calling complaining about his satellite giving him problems."

He snapped his finger three times trying to get his partner's attention that was drinking from a hot Sprite glitter bottle.

"Sounds like our friend has company." Turning the volume up inside the audio headset he could hear the relaxed knocks at the front door.

Hearing the unexpected knock at the door the Haitian tiptoed to the peephole.

"Who dat on my door?" He said with a deep Haitian accent.

"Direct TV."

"Me not like TV dem got de wrong apartment!" Looking through the peephole he could see Officer

Dixon in classical police position with his glock .19 in his hand.

"What the fuck is Direct TV doing at the door? The agent looking through the tripod said. Looking at the culprit running toward the bag of money he filled up knocking over a glass flower vase on the table.

Hearing the glass shattering on the other side of the door Officer Hill kicked the door in.

"DEA mutherfucker!" Before he could finish he was diving to the floor. The fearless beast had nothing to lose. Emptying the .357 of every bullet it could carry.

Boom Boom Just missing Officer Hill. Sending Officer Dixon flying through the air.

Looking through the lens, the agent could see the culprit running toward the closet searching for a bigger weapon. Coming away with a P89. Seeing him return fire into the other room he thought it was a stick up. Zooming through the apartment he could see Officer Dixon reloading his weapon behind a flipped over couch with plaster and drywall all over his face and hair.

He zoomed through the hallway he could see Officer Hill returning fire into the room where the shots were coming from. Taking the lens back into the bedroom he could see the criminal opening the window that led to the fire escape.

He zoomed back into the hallway he could see the DEA badge hanging from Officer Hill's neck.

"You have to come look at this. What the fuck is DEA doing in there?" The black Internal Affairs agent grabbing a part of 10x50 60mm binoculars.

Agent Dixon had been shot in the left leg. He was in pain trying to reload his glock. His left arm was going numb from the gun womb.

Boom Boom Boom Boom Sending Agent Hill front flipping into the room across from the Haitian was. Agent Hill sending shots back. Screaming as he unloaded his artillery, sending a storm of bullets in the Haitian's direction.

The two Internal Affairs agents stood in the window 500 feet away looking at the clatter taking place. Soon as the criminal got one foot on the middle of the fire escape, he lost his balanced causing him to lose possession of his weapon, sending it free falling to the pavement below.

"Fuck!" He said looking at his weapon fall. Agent Hill was hot on his ass sending two shots through the door. Bullets colliding with the glass of the window. Specks of glass cut the Haitian's. Agent Dixon was trying to get up. You could hear the Haitian's weapon hitting the metal stairs on its freefall to the pavement. Agent Hill was like the Terminator kicking the door opened with one motion with his adrenaline.

"Don't move asshole!" With both hands on his pistol looking through his target. The duffle bag was enabling the suspect to exit what was left of the window. Agent Hill jumped on the suspect's back catching a strong elbow sending him stumbling three feet backwards with the duffle bag in his hand, ripping a hole in the side of the bag from the force of his grip. Officer Hill no longer needed to apply pressure after coming into contact with the bag of drug money, he started stuffing money every place he could. When he ran to the window he could see the culprit jumping onto a blue dumpster. Making sure the scene was clear he emptied the remainder of bullets left in his pistol, and then smashed his head through the window. Officer Dixon entered the room limping with blood running down his leg and his arm still gripping his glock.

"Did you get him?"

"That son of a bitch put up a mean fight."

The case manager called C-low into her office. It was time for his six month unit review with his unit team. He had turned down the drug program. He could not take anybody telling him it was something wrong with his thinking and that he had a drug problem. But truth be told he was making fifteen grand a month.

He and the captain's wife got lost in their emotions. Over the past few weeks he found himself catching feelings for her. When he transferred to McKean one of his partners got him a job inside the commissary warehouse. At the time the captain's wife was the head CO inside the warehouse two years ago.

"Look Ms. Thomas it's no need to keep asking about taking the drug program. I'm going to finish up my time the way I been doing it. I do not want any halfway house. I can care less about getting any time off from you white folks. If that was the case I would of been home."

Chapter Fourteen

15 Years Ago

Sam walked inside Pedro's place of business. His face was red as the floors of hell. He was a wreck emotionally.

"Diamond been missing for three months with that pimp Day-Day. He got my wife prostituting and hoeing likes she a piece of shit. You need to do something about it before I take matters into my own hands!"

Pedro put his cigar down and slowly spun around in his chair. Facing the rookie cop staring him down him could see Sam's soul. He grabbed him by the neck assertively throwing him on top of the marble desk.

"Don't you ever come in my fucking establishment and tell me what to do. Next time I will make sure I break your fucking neck. You need to check your bitch!" He said releasing his grip.

"Now listen the tables always turn. One day we gone need Day-Day. In the meanwhile you have the upper hand. The next time you see her let that be the last time anybody sees her." He said fixing Sam's collar on his police uniform. To tell the truth Pedro was using Diamond against Sam. He knew he would need Sam and his ties to the police to keep his blocks running the way he expected them to run. He put Day-Day on Diamond to keep Sam around. He had it mapped out. If Day-Day did not want to pay his 20%. Then he was going to have Diamond killed and let Sam book him for kidnapping and murder. *To tell the truth she did have some good pussy* Pedro thought to himself.

By Pedro having dark hair people thought he was African American until he spoke of violence every time he spoke. It was corruption and drugs that built his family legacy. Sam came into his office at the wrong time. He was dealing with his father's one year anniversary of his death. His family had inherited a lifelong drug rival with the Santana cartel. That was not going to stop until Santana or Pedro was put to death.

When Pedro moved from Miami to Cleveland, he settled into a small apartment on the south side of town. Looking out the window he could see how different the drug trade was operating in Cleveland. The structure was more of pimps and players. In Miami it was cartels and extortion.

Lil' Jimmy was always out on the block in front of his building. No matter how early of late it was Jimmy was posted. It was no major connect around for him to invest the little bit of money he was making.

One day the police and street vice raided the strip. Hearing a knock at the door he was astound to see a out of breath Jimmy. He had swallowed five rocks in the process of fleeing from the law enforcement. Pedro took Jimmy under his wing from that day on. Showing him how to run a cartel instead of a block. He was in junior high school when Pedro helped enhance his position in the drug trade.

Jimmy was at difference with a young fifteen year old ticking bomb who wanted in on Jimmy operation by the name of Greedy or he was going to take it all.

Jimmy had a stash house that he checked every Friday at the same time. Greedy had been laying on him for about two months finally getting the right opportunity he took advantage. Soon as Jimmy put the key in the door he could hear the sound of Greedy glock being cocked. Pressing the cold steel against the back of his head walking him inside.

"I tried everything in the book. You think they call me Greedy because I'm greedy? It's because niggas like you that's greedy and want everything for you self. You just had to get greedy on me didn't you?" *Boom Boom Boom*

He did not even let Jimmy's body hit the ground before he was searching the house for what he came for. Nobody knew who killed Jimmy. Greedy got away with five kilos of Peruvian flake. Pedro was not concerned about the death of his protégé. He respected the game and understood the power of the streets. He knew his product would hit the streets in due time.

Greedy was blocked in by two black SUVs. With three guns facing him they pulled him out of his car. He was thrown in the back of the truck. Feeling the overweight SUV gaining momentum. The lengthy ride was unexpected as well as the unknown of his future.

Hearing a commercial garage door open he felt the vehicle come to a conclusion. He could hear a conversation but could not understand Spanish.

Pedro positioned two lawn chairs directly across from each other in the middle of the room under a light fixture. The environment was moist and cold. You couldn't hear a sound and you could smell the smoke that filled the once fresh air. Pedro pulled his chair a little closer to Greedy's.

"Do you know why it is that you are here?" Looking befuddled Greedy did not muster a word.

"Well young man I respect you to the fullest. Unfortunately you have something that belongs to me. Lucky for you there is options." He said blowing the smoke from the cigar in Greedy's face.

"You can return my product back to me that was not yet paid for or pay the price I gave it to Jimmy for. Or you can take your last breath inside this warehouse. Hearing the sound of the gunmen's weapons being cocked back did not put fear inside Greedy's eyes. It only installed vengeance in his eyes. Greedy looked Pedro deep in his cold eyes.

"Now I'm going to give you some options. You can kill me right here. Or you can pick your money up that I already made of your product. Or you can be my coke connect." He said as he stuck his hand out to embrace the unknown.

"Can you fucking believe this fucking kid?" Pedro said laughingly as he choked from the pollution that clogged his lungs.

"I like him!"

Burt let his good childhood friend Shoe Shine set up shop inside the restroom of his club on nights it was open to the public. Shoe Shine fail victim to the needle at a young age. On the night the club would have a good night, Shoe Shine provided candy, cologne and toothbrushes for the gentlemen that were drunk. He even shined their expensive gator shoes. Burt had won the club gambling. Ox was 13 at the time when Burt took him under his wing. He saw Santana and his brother coming through the entrance of the club. Burt made sure he paid extra attention to the unfamiliar faces that just popped up out of the blue. He knew they were out of towners from their taste of fabric and jewelry. Santana had to relief himself to the restroom. Two cavilers where all over the two brother's movements. They made their way through the thick night crowd to the restroom. Santana made it to an empty stall just in the nick of time. His brother was washing his hands making small conversation with Shoe Shine. Shaking the last drops of fluid from his hands, he never observed the villain stab him in his back with a six inch pocket knife. He was taken by surprise when the other villain jumped on his back trying to get his 14k gold necklace from around his neck. He was beating him inadequately. His brother jumped in. Burt and a few of his club security penetrated through the commotion putting in revengeful work on the two unwanted.

"Take these two to my office and get them cleaned up." Seeing Ox inside the offices at a young age at this time of night, Santana knew he held significant value for his age. Saving Santana and his brother Burt was rewarded with unlimited coke. He had met one of the finest drug cartel from the bottom of the map, until they found out about his gambling habits.

Chapter Fifthteen

Graduation

"Let today's graduates become tomorrow's leaders. Let the Northern High class of 2003 hold their heads up high and progress through life with confidence."

Bud was in deep thought when he saw Larry enter the auditorium with to red bones. Within a short period of time he managed to gain all his weight back.

He was proud of Bud. It was because of him he quit smoking and wanted to live a clean life again.

"Man where the hell you been at?" He said looking at Larry up and down.

"I had to get myself together. I needed some time to get my life back on track. After we came back from Buffalo it seemed like you had more faith in me then I had in myself. So I checked into rehab. That was my way of saying thanks to you for keeping it 100 with me. I remember back in 1977 when I got my first hoe. The pimp she was working for said something to me I will never forget. He said young blood you think you rich and smart but down the line you gone realize you was broke and dumb. At the time I did not understand what the hell he was talking about. When I was sitting in that cold ass room in rehab, it all came together what he was saying to me. I want you to remember something. Just because you see an old drunk or junkie on the playground bench that does not mean he has nothing to offer. I'm proud of you." Larry said giving Bud a passionate hug.

"I respect all the game you give me bruh. I just invested in a building on the west side last week. Soon as you come across the bridge. YOU STAY CLEAN! I will help you get on your feet. I will even help you get a van and start you a small car wash on wheels. Just do me one favor stay clean!"

Ty and Lamika had been seeing each other off and on over the past few months. They were driving east on Clark Avenue when his cell phone sounded off. He checked his caller ID and saw it was Officer Dixon's number. He did not want to answer.

"Yo!"

"Ty we will meet you inside Friday's parking lot downtown in the Flats at 11:00 tomorrow night about your next transaction." His face was full of fulminate listening to Officer Dixon's voice. Ty turned the music up so Lamika could not hear his conversation.

"Look like I told you, this is the wrong person to rush. I'm telling you if he feels any kind of heat it's a wrap!"

Officer Dixon cut him off, "Don't be late!"

"What's wrong?" Lamika asked.

"Just the same old street shit." He said pulling into Long John Silver's restaurant.

Matt was coming from Big Lots with his mother when he spotted Ty inside the drive thru. He made a U-turn in the middle of traffic making sure his mind wasn't playing tricks on him.

"What the hell are you doing?" His mother asked in a pertinent voice. He pulled up on the side of the vehicle.

"So you two have finally finished school. What's next?"

"Well Mr. Clark I just invested into a building on the lower west side. I'm looking to convert it into a barber shop and beauty salon. I plan to open it up after I complete Barber College. By that time, Trina should be finishing up her last few months of nursing school."

Lil' Bud had taken a cat nap on his grandmother Cookie saggy breast as usual.

"Pete slow down my nigga you gone pass the exit up!" Nutt spoke.

Pete and Nutt exited Wooster Blvd with the intent for the big take out on Nutt's sister's brother's friend in Akron, Ohio. Pulling into Edgewood Projects, Nutt had to remember which apartment it was.

"Slow down my nigga!" Nutt said sitting on the edge of the passenger's seat. His vision was blurred from the incessant of blunts.

"That's it right there with the light on."

Nutt knocked on the door aggressively. A female voice arose from behind the door.

"Who is it?"

"It's Slim from out West!"

"Who?"

Boom Pete kicked in what was a door.

"You asking too much bitch!" He said snatching the female who answered the door by her naturally long jet black hair. She could feel blood rushing to the right side of her head from Pete impenetrable grip.

Inside the apartment was two middle aged male adults and two females who appeared to be in their late teens. Nutt positioned the other female inside a choke hold. He took her hostage, aiming the chrome .357 at her temple.

Pete landed a hard blow to the back of the female head causing her to blackout. Focusing his firearm at the two victims. One of the privy was not having it.

"Don't move mutherfucka!" He said in an arduous tone gripping his weapon tighter. He was not hearing Pete at all. He was trying to get to his handgun from under the loveseat. Pete hit him with a back shot.

"Ah! This nigga shot me!" He said talking through his teeth. The impact opened the victim back up hastily. Leaving him face down on the floor in a puddle of warm blood. Seeing her brother laid out the teenager Nutt was taking hostage started yelling and kicking.

"Shut the fuck up!" He flexed his manly strength around her frail neck. Nutt choked her out. Nutt and Pete did not realize it was a six year old boy scared to death overlooking the squall from the top of the stairs.

"Fuck with me if you want to nigga. Now tell me what I want to hear or yo as is grass." He said aiming his 12 gauge in the direction of the last victim standing.

"Look man what ever happen just don't kill me. My son is upstairs. I got 30 pounds of weed and fifty stacks in my bedroom you can have it all just don't shoot me!"

Mr. Floyd was having a warm cup of green tea with a fresh cut lemon when he seen two mask gunmen fleeing from out of Carlos' weed house with two portmanteaus in their dominion. Carlos had the projects on smash for the last five years with his interdicted involvements in the weed trade. Mr. Floyd could see the blood that stained the unlawful cavaliers.

Big Mike picked his communication line up on the fourth ring. It was Tammy. She and Big Mike had been doing business for the last five months. With the help of her younger brother she was able to establish a foundation on 117th and St. Clair on the seller's end of the block. She had a steady flow of customers coming through her trap house. Tammy purchased a half of kilo every three to four days.

"What's good Tammy? I thought you forgot my number. I have not heard from you in a few days."

"I can't call it Big Mike if the timing is right I need to see you."

"Same way as last time?"

"You can come all the way this time."

"Say no more I will call you in about ten minutes."

Lil' Tone had been calling Lamika all day still no answer. She had him pussy whipped. It was nothing nobody could do or say to bring him back down to earth. Once Lamika learned that her pussy was power. She planned to use that to her advantage.

Tone was sitting on the hood of his black on black 68 442 Cutlass eating a bag of plain Ruffles chips and drinking a Lipton's Iced Tea inside Whitmore's parking lot. Watching a few local cats he grew up with in the community playing four five and six on the side of the brick red building on 143rd and Kinsman Avenue when the vice pulled up.

This was Clip's sixth time calling PW.

"God damn bruh you said you was about to pull up ten minutes ago. I'm missing all kinds of money waiting on you out here."

"Quit crying, I'm looking at you right now. I'm coming up Lockyear." Traffic was compact inside the small plaza located on the corner of 79th street and Money Avenue. It was a great division of land.

So many styles of people were attracted to the plaza from low life wine heads and high school dropouts. The mini mart pulled in some business for the ones who wanted to cash their checks. Goldie's fish and chicken stayed open until midnight every night. The clothing store set at the end of the plaza. A lot of the smokers enjoyed the underworld environment because there was always work around to keep their addiction going. PW was nowhere near Lockyear. He pushed Shanda's head back down.

Tammy phone rang. It was Big Mike.

"I'm making a left on 117th Street right now."

This was Big Mike's first time coming to her trap house on Sellers. Coming to a complete stop at the stop sign at the corner of 117th Street and Sellers He didn't pay attention to small crowd posted in front of the corner store slap boxing and smoking blunts. It was two middle aged youth teenaged competitors trying to beat each other out for a twenty dollar sale from a local smoker, who pulled up in front of the store as he was making a right hand turn. He wasn't paying any attention to the two misfits on the payphone on the far end of the store building.

He reached in his back seat for the half of kilo inside the City Blue shopping bag. Up under the passenger's seat was two Subway bags filled with twenty stacks. He hit the speed dial.

"Tammy come outside I'm in the driveway."

When Big Mike entered the house, Tammy was walking around in some all-black boy shorts and a wife beater. Her hair was in a-ponytail. She was not bad looking for her age. Big Mike had to give it to her; she still had a nice shape for someone pushing 40 years of age.

"You should not be walking around the house like that when it's time to do business."

"It's always business for me. Since when has it been anything else? I know you want some of this pussy Mike."

He changed subjects seeing where the conversation was going.

"Look I only have half of what you wanted. I was already in traffic when you called me. I can take care of the other half first thing in the morning."

"You always got some shit with you. Yo phatt ass need to quit playing so much when it comes to money."

Two jack boys positioned their self inside the dark hallway that awaited their victim. Tammy's brother hopped in the back seat of his still running vehicle.

"Look Tammy I left my car running. Just answer your phone first thing in the morning."

The other gunman was standing at the bus stop on Eddy Road as a look out. Big Mike put the money in his pocket from the transaction and walked towards the door he once entered in.

"Don't forget to call me either,"

PW pulled inside the Jump Off parking lot a half hour later. He saw Clip through the glass window of-the clothing store counter dialogue with Arab Venny. He hopped out the car just to style on the young up and coming D boys whose shoes he once was in on the same ugly corners. Hitting the glass window putting both his arms in the air indicating Venny to buzz him in. Once inside the store PW brought so much energy, changing the atmosphere.

"Venny what's up baby?" He said giving his good friend dap.

"Young Clips what's the deal bruh?"

"I got five hundred for you bruh."

"Bet, let me get some fresh white tees."

"Yo!" V let me get a case of 3X white tees."

"Clips meet me in the car; let me take care of Venny."

"Venny what you for them?"

"Well you know me, just give me a fifty sack of some good weed and we even."

"That's love bruh. I'm going to send it back in with Clips."

When the fresh air hit PW, he was greeted with a rush. Nobody had any product. Usually Pete would be around, but it was no need to miss any money. PW loved the rush. This was one of the main reasons he missed being on the strip. It was moments and days like that, that he missed. The hood always showed him love and he made sure he kept that love they displayed for him. When he sat in the car, he was sweating just a little bit. He turned the AC up to cool off.

"Clips you in a rush?"

"Naw why, what's up?"

"You feel like twisting up."

"I don't care."

"Shanda look inside the glove box and hand me that scale out of there and them sandwich bags?"

"Give me a light bruh."

"Damn nigga that was fast as hell. That's for you my nigga. Give this sack to Venny for me. You said you got a soft nick. This what I'm going to do for you. Give me that five hundred and take this two and a split and hit me up when you get right my nigga."

"That's why I fuck with you. You always make sure a nigga right. I don't give a damn what happen. If you need me nigga fo anything I'm hear fo you!"

Big Mike was reaching for his ringing cell phone in his back pocket.

"Shut up pussy ass nigga!" The jack-boy said pressing the cold steel against Big Mike's head.

"Now act up if you want to! Blow yo head smooth off nigga. You can make this shit hard or you can make this shit easy, it's on you!" He said hitting Big Mike in the back of the head with the pistol.

The two local vice detectives hopped out the car dressed in plan street clothes with their police badge hanging around their necks.

"So this how y'all doing now. Just saying fuck it ha. You see this shit!" He said talking to his partner.

"They gone disrespect us like this in public dice game!"

"Get against the car you mutherfucker know the procedure!" Tone ignored the direct order and kept eating his hot wings he ordered.

"So that's how we playing it now ha Antonio!" The driver said throwing Tone's food to the ground.

"Say something! You want to be like yo big brother now ha? I'm going to make sure you end up just like him. Get up against the car fuck you think you is!"

Pete and Nutt pulled into Peaches' apartment complex on 71st and Wade Park to split the money and the weed they just came up on. Peaches walked in twenty minutes later. Nutt had just left. He did not feel like hearing her mouth about him being with Nutt.

Pete and Peaches had an apartment and a two bedroom house out in UppetyHeights. The apartment was the first thing he invested into after they had met.

"So what good?" Pete asked flicking through the channels on the flat screen.

"Nigga quit playing. I been knowing you long enough to know when you up to something. You only talk like that when you want some pussy." Pete bust out into guffaw.

"Girl you crazy. I wonder how you sound when you want something. Looking around you have a lot. Two spots both of them plushed out and you always fly."

"You damn right and you gone make sure my houses is plushed out and I stay fly."

"So what's the deal on slim from up the way?"

"I have not talked to him in a few days, but he will call this weekend if I do not talk to him."

"Look, want you get dressed so we can catch a movie or something."

On the way home, Bud's cell phone rang.

"Hello?"

"What's good, can I speak to Bud?"

"This me. Bud said looking over at Trina.

"It's Shanell I was calling to see what you was up too."

"I'm on my way back home. I just came from dinner with my family. If it's cool I can hit you back tomorrow."

"That's cool with me."

"Or you can stop by the college if you want a haircut. I should be in around 11:00." Bud said giving her the read between the line conversation.

"I hope you ain't trying to talk in no codes in my face Bud!"

"Girl stop trippin!"

"Don't get fucked up in this car Bud! I been with you long enough! Play with me if you want to!"

"Girl that was a customer for tomorrow. You going crazy. I do not know what they put in that food but you trippin." He said hitting the steering wheel laughing at Trina.

"Oh you think it's funny! Let me find out Bud!"

The two lovebirds pulled up to Lamika's apartment at the same time as Lamika and Ty. Bud was so deep into it with Trina he did not even pay any attention
to Lamika exiting out of Ty's vehicle.

Soon as Ty pulled of Officer Dixon called him.

"Meet us at location AWOL in one hour."

"What the hell is wrong with y'all two?" Ty said walking inside the building.

"Yo cousin think he slick. He got the nerve to have another bitch call his phone."

"Girl stop crying he ain't going nowhere."

"Don't be trying to take his side."

Bud set in the car. He had other things on his mind. The State Board was in three days. Plus he was down to his last thirty grand after buying the building. He was down to his last twenty pounds and five pounds of haze. When he was riding through Whitewood Ohio he saw a nice house he wanted to check into. He knew getting his barber and beauty salon open and the nice house he was going to have to get his hands back dirty. He needed two hundred stacks. His self-talk was, *I'm not going to any clubs or smoking no weed until I reach my goal.* He said to himself closing the door to his SUV.

Chapter Sixteen

What's Next

Bud parked his old school in front of the door.

"Damn nigga, that's how you feel?" Young Al from the Kingston projects said cleaning his clippers.

"New whip!"

"I had that car last summer. I just don't drive it."

"What them is twenty-twos?"

"Yea on the front and twenty-fours on the back."

"So what you into you can keep it 100 with me."

"Man I just cut hair." He said pulling his clippers from his bag.

"Come on now Bud who you think you fooling?"

Pulling Al to the side.

"Look Bruh I sell a little weed here and there."

Al enrolled into Barber College two months ago he comes when he wants. Shanell tiptoed through the door at 11:30 with her son.

"I see you got yo lil' mans with you. You doing a good job with him."

"I try; it's hard being a single parent out here."

"What up Shanell." Al spoke on his way to his station.

"You two know each other."

"Me and Al grew up together. He from Case projects."

Al had been flirting with her for years. She never gave him the time of day. She had no time to waste when it came to dealing with cats from the hood.

"I mean he cool he just ain't my type." Looking at Bud, letting him know just what her type is.

"How you want me to cut his hair this time?"

"Cut it the same way; just take it a little lower. I think you cut it like that so I would have a reason to bring him back quicker."

"You think I would do something like that." He said tying the back of the smock.

"I see you were busy last night when I called. I liked how you rushed me off the phone." She said in a gentle tone of voice.

"Yea I was coming from dinner with my girl when you called."

"You never told me you had a girlfriend."

"You never asked." He said looking up to make eye contact.

"Look! I'm about to take my lunch break at 12:30 you up for lunch?"

"That's cool with me. I have to take him to daycare then I'm free."

Washing his hands in the sink on the back bar. He heard his name over the intercom.

Inside the barber instructor's office he took a seat in the wooded leather chair.

"Well young man two days away instead of two months. You are one of the best I done seen come through these doors in a long time. I have three Cavs' tickets for next month's game against the Lakers. Here, they yours. They are not front row, but you will be able to see the players and hear the conversation from their bench."

PW was the last person Big Mike talked to before going to see Tammy. He was still sleep when he heard his cell phone ringing in his pants pocket.

"Yea nigga! If you want this phatt greasy nigga to live you better come up with ticket straight cash nothing less then, a half a million dollars. If you know like I know you better leave the police out of this. I will call in two days."

Bud called Shanell and informed her to meet him at the Fifth Wheel restaurant located on 26th Avenue. She was getting out of her car when Bud pulled up. She did not suspect a well put together muscle car to belong to him.
Bud left his cell phone in the car so it could charge up. The Fifth Wheel was home to some of the best breakfast food in the city.

Pete had just finished dicking down Peaches. He was in the shower when she handed him the phone.

"They got em bruh!"

"Got who? What the hell you talking about?" He said stepping one leg out of the shower so he could hear what PW was talking about.

"Big Mike! Somebody kidnapped him. They want a half a ticket."

"Look! Meet me on the Duce!"

When Bud positioned himself back inside his car he had thirty missed calls all from PW. He called him back.

"Yo what up bruh?"

"Shit just got real! I need you to meet me on the Duce!" Hearing the convulsion in his voice he know something bad taking place.

When Pete and Bud pulled up PW was smoking a blunt.

"What the hell you talking about they got Big Mike and who got him!" A bewildered Bud said.

"It's all bad! Somebody called and woke me up saying if I want to keep him alive I need to come up with a half a ticket. He said he was going to call back in two days then he hung up."

"Who hung up?"

"Look I don't fucking know nigga! I'm in the dark just like y'all. I don't know what the fuck is going on."

"What the fuck we gone do, because I know fo damn sho we do not have a half a ticket." Bud spoke taking a seat on the six inch curb.

"Don't even trip. I got something for us." Pete said with a barbarous look in his eyes.

"Pete what the fuck is you thinking bruh." PW asked with his hands in his pocket.

"We going for the big takeout!"

"What!"

"We gone hit a bank!"

"Nigga is you fucking serious!" Bud stood up.

"Nigga it's do or die y'all either in or y'all out. I can't let Big Mike death be on my hands. It's crunch time. Look give me until tomorrow. I got somebody who works at the bank we can hit. I will call y'all tomorrow with the blue print. We will meet up at Peaches' spot. Make sure y'all niggas clear y'all head before tomorrow."

PW and Bud was lost for words when Pete pulled off.

"I have to call Larry."

"Fuck you talking about! Ain't nobody seen him in about a year."

"Larry was in rehab. Something like this. I can't leave him in the dark about this."

Deon noticed he was being superseded by an all-black Ford Explorer. He felt it was odd for him to be the one being followed. For the last few weeks his operation

151

has been shut down. Being robbed was the last thing on his mind.

"Yo Ice make a left and see if this truck is following us." The all-black truck made a left as well.

"Hit the freeway and pull inside a random parking lot. We gone leave this van in the underground garage, hop out and hit the train."

"Suspect heading East on interstate 90." Officer Dixon listened over the scanner as the two federal agents superseding Deon and his comrades.

Two internal affairs agents walked in to the small office that officer Dixon was positioned in. He had his left leg elevated on a chair.-He suffered severe nerve damage from the gunshot wound a few months back. His left arm was still in a sling.

"Long time no see Officer Dixon. How's your rehab going?"

"I'm taking it one day at a time."

"You know you would have never been in that situation if your partner had not been so greedy. Speaking of the devil where is he?"

"Suspect entering Tower City parking garage. Three suspects exiting the vehicle."

"Look like you are on to something. So whose idea was it to raid that Haitian's apartment that day? Yours or His?"

"I don't know what you are talking about."

"Listen we know how hard it is being a rookie agent. Especially with a partner like yours. We know that you are in the dark about a lot of things that your partner is involved in. In due time you will come around. You take care of yourself young man." He knocked on the desk before leaving out the office.

Officer Dixon was in a confused state of mind. He did not know what the hell the two internal affair agents were talking about. Five hours later the agent's voice registered over the scanner.

"We lost them!"

"Fuck!" He said slamming the scanner to the floor. He limped out the office. He punched the wall with his free hand.

Deon and his comrades threw all their phones inside a trashcan before riding the train. Deon advised them to turn them on before trashing them before going their separate ways.

Peaches was doing Trina's hair inside Lamika's kitchen when Tone walked in.

"Yea I heard y'all in here talking about how niggas ain't shit." They all started laughing.

"What's so crazy y'all got the nerve to have Lil' BJ in here listening to this BS." He said picking Little Bud up.

"God damn when was the last time you change this lil' nigga? Smell like a grown man." He said putting him back down.

Meanwhile

Pete knew April would come in handy one day. That day finally came. Sitting at the dining room table was Pete, Larry, Bud, PW, Nutt, and Starr. Pete laid the blueprint out of the bank on the table. Giving every one of his affiliates instructions.

Pete was going over every detail to make sure everybody would move as one. Once inside the bank April informed him after five o'clock-it would only be one security guard they had to deal with.

"Look, at 5:45 we hitting Key Bank on 105th and Money, no ifs,-ands or buts about it."

Starr looked everybody in the eye to make sure she was not dealing with anybody to weak for the mission. Pete threw a black bag on the table. Inside the bag was everything they needed to pull the job off. He gave everybody a ski mask and a salt and pepper wig.

Chapter Seventeen

5:45PM

The bank was uncomfortably crowded. The fact that is was closing time did not delay what was to take place.

Starr walked in dressed like a middle aged school teacher with an oversized blond wig on. She scanned the guts of the bank. She located all the cameras making sure the red lights were turned off, thanks to April. It was a line of customers at the ATM machine and at each of the five teller windows. It was even a few people standing in a commercial account line.

The security guard was a-well put together thirty four year old ex-navy seal. He was walking around tapping his flashlight in the palm of his right hand. Starr entered the bank's restroom and found an empty stall. She pulled out her cell phone. She sent Pete a text message, giving him the green light.

Looking at his watch they had two minutes until show time.

"Hi!" She heard a child's voice say. Starr looked down and saw a little white girl staring up at her. She put on a fake smile.

"Hello."

"My stepmother is a cop." The girl stated.

"Is that so?"

"Uum." She said pointing to the black lady, well in shape like Jackie Brown. She was standing at the counter filling out a deposit slip.

"There she is right there. She's the best!"

The girl's voice faded out. Starr lowered her glasses, watching the lady closely.

Her back up revolver was bulging out her tight fitted cop coat. How could she have missed something as crucial as that? The lady's face had cop all over it. Looking at her watch it was 5:45 on the head.

Damn too late to call it off.

"Her and daddy are getting married-soon!" The little girl voice registered again.

"Did you hear me?"

"Huh yes, yes I heard you." She said as she walked off as the little girl stuck her tongue out at Starr. The cop was having a difficult time filling out the deposit slip. She was on her third one. Starr snuck up behind her and smiled continuing what she was doing she watched her mess up another slip before offering her a helping hand.

"Excuse me." She said tapping the lady cop on the shoulder. She turned around.

"Do you need any help?"

Pete hung up the pay phone outside the bank when he seen the getaway vehicle pulling off. Humanity outside the bank and around the area was too busy to see the three masked gunmen walking in the direction of the bank.

They were five feet away from the entrance when Pete slipped in before them. The security guard was trying to lock the door.

"Excuse me sir we're closing!" Pete hit him with the Taser gun.

"Make an exception!" He said as the guard's limp body fell to the floor.

Larry dragged him off to the side and duck taped his feet and hands. Nutt passed Pete with an AK-47 in his hand on his way over to one of the teller windows.

Teller at window four tensed up when she seen Larry rushing in her direction with a pistol in his hand. She went for the emergency button. He pointed his gun in her face.

"Don't do it! Remove your finger from the button bitch!"

The crowd heads turned from the sound of Nutt's voice. Seeing the big machine gun in his hand sent them- into a panic.

"Aaah!" Screaming came from each corner of the bank. Larry took one side and Pete took the other side. Nutt jumped on the counter.

"Everybody down on the floor now!"-Brandishing his weapon. People did as they were told. Some was not moving fast enough.

Pete snatch the lady cop stepdaughter up.

"Do it or she gets it!"

Nutt handed black-bags to all the tellers.

"Fill em! No funny money. Let's go! Hurry the fuck up!"

The cop hesitated as she slowly got down on the floor. Starr waited for her to comply before she got down. The cop kept one hand above her head and the other one on her .38-inside her blazer's pocket.

April stood silent praying that everything went as planned. She almost shitted on herself seeing Pete coming her way.

"You!" Pete said pointing.

"Come with me!" He said snatching her by the collar, dragging her to the vault.

The police officer felt helpless lying their watching her scared stepdaughter. She was facing the wall with her hand up counting backwards from a hundred.-

Pete told her if she hit zero before they finished she would be punished for cheating. Nutt tossed a bag of money to Larry from teller two's window.

"Let's go! Fill them fucking bags up!" The lady cop's partner that was on the floor, felt it was the perfect time to make his move. He gazed over at his partner.

Office Tillman was on the floor by teller five. She gave Tillman the head nod to make his move. He jumped up and drew his .38 revolver.

"Police nobody move!" He ordered aiming his weapon at Larry. Larry had his gun already pointed at officer Tillman. The lady cop on the floor next to Starr rose to her feet drawing her gun.

"Drop em!"

"Larry move!" Officer Tillman removed his gun from Larry taking a shot at Nutt.

Pow Pow Nutt dove behind the counter where teller one was. By the time Officer Tillman turned back around it was too late, Larry had the ups on him. Just as he was about to squeeze the trigger he was hit with an arm shot from across the room. Before the lady cop could take one more shot she felt the cold- steal from Starr's .40 Cal lowered in her back.

Boom Boom A speck of blood landed on Starr's face from the close range shot.
The crowd started running in all directions trying to free themselves. Hearing the crowd getting louder the little girl closed her eyes tighter and continued counting. Pete ran and checked on Larry. Officer Tillman peeked behind the desk. He did not see Starr crouched low and sending hot mental in his direction.

Boom Boom

"Abort! Abort!" Starr yelled over the gun shots and screams.-Inside her walkie talkies. Pete was helping Larry off the floor.-Sirens could be heard. Nutt had finished collecting the four bags of money from the rest of the tellers when he had a clean shot on officer Tillman reloading his revolver. Aiming his AK-47 at his head he pulled the trigger, decapitating his head from his shoulders. His police radio fell to the floor. Pete picked it up on the way out.

"Radio dispatch fuck the police!" He said crushing the radio heading for the exit.

Just as they were exiting out the bank a black unmarked crown Victoria pulled up in front of the bank. The two detectives did not have a chance to stop the car.

Nutt and Pete unloaded on the vehicle raining bullets hitting the metals like cotton.

"Come on Starr!" Yelled Larry. They sprinted in the direction of East-99th taking them to the Blvd. Starr's adrenaline was pumping so fast she came close to getting caught.

Another car pulled-up trying to cut them off. The driver jumped out using his door as a shield as he pointed his Glock.

Boom Boom Boom Boom

Starr sent the remainder of her bullets through the driver's window forcing him to fall backwards on the pavement. The suspects made their escape hitting the Blvd hopping in the dirty creak water.

"Man this water stinks!" Nutt said.

"Shut up and run damnit!" Starr yelled before her heel broke on her dress shoe, causing her to fall face first in the water.

Pete ran into her looking back to make sure everybody was still together. He pulled her up out of the water.

"Take them heels off!"

"I have too many bags to carry you!"

Sirens could be heard from all directions. Reaching and opening. They could hear the powerful motor from the getaway car roaring.

Bud saw all the police cars and helicopters patrolling the area. He was too far from the bank to see what was going on. When he heard the gun shot his first mind told him, *if they had any kind of sense they would hit the boulevard.*-Seconds later he pulled up to the bottom of Snake Hill.

Larry and Nutt hid in the trunk. Pete laid face down in the back seat. Starr position herself low in the front seat. Coming to the top of the hill, Bud was at the stop sign across from the old Peacock corner store. By the time he got to Styles of Success beauty salon, a police car pulled next to him going the other direction with his nose in the air. Bud shot him a fuck you look and sped off. Nutt and Larry felt the car come to a halt.

The occupants exited the vehicle. Bud tossed Nutt the keys.

"Get rid of this car!" He said walking inside the building.

Ain't No Love in the City

Pete and Starr was sitting on the floor separating the money when PW called. "Yo bruh it's about that time!"

PW pulled up to the back of Glenville High School with two duffle bags. Each bag contained two hundred and fifty thousand dollars apiece.

They placed the two bags of money inside a metal garbage can. When they took the lid off they seen Big Mike's Air Max 95s.

His phone rang.

"Now leave! We will call you once we finish counting the money!"

Pete and Bud was waiting for PW to pull back up with Big Mike. All their dreams were shattered when they saw PW pull back up by his self.

Bud insides started bubbling. Just as PW was exiting the car his cell phone rang again.

"Come get this phatt funky as nigga! You can meet us at the Boys and Girls Club in the parking lot on Broadway!"

When they pulled up the crowd was congested. Pete could not stomach what he was seeing. Police had the parking-lot blocked off. Fox 8 news team was present on the crime scene. Big Mike was shot six times, three to the head and three to the chest.

One of the employees found him naked-when she came to work. Fox 8 News team was interviewing her live, when Bud exited the car. The death of Big Mike came across the TV screen inside while Granny D was at work. The three hustlers was tormented. They did not know who would do such a thing. On top of that they hit the bank and Big Mike still got killed.

The funeral-was jammed pack to see one of Eight Duce finest laid to rest. Granny D had took a devastating blow emotionally. In the past four years she has laid two of her sons to rest.

After the funeral, Pete and Bud-sent her back down south for a while with distance kinfolks, so she could get a piece of mind.

Ty pulled out the drive way to meet Officer Hill and Dixon at Page Town mobile phone store, inside the plaza on Lorain Avenue on the west side of Cleveland.

Ty had too much on his mind to realize he was being followed by an all-white Dodge Ram pickup truck.

When Ty pulled-inside the plaza to meet the two agents, the driver of the Ram truck was in range.

"This rat as nigga!" They said hitting the steering column.

Ox was showing Tone the ins and outs of the coke game when his phone rang.

"Hey baby what's up. Long time no hear from."

"Yea I been kind of busy." He said adding cold water to the glue like substance inside the glass Pyrex.

"I'm going to swing by their later on!" Trying to rush Starr off the phone he replied.

"Don't forget either!"

Since the bank robbery the team was laying low. Bud finally finished Barber College. His shop was still under construction. They were relaxing at Lamika's apartment reminiscencing about Big Mike. PW, Larry, Pete and Bud.

Still in the dark about who killed Big Mike, seemed to bother them every one of them.

Pete was looking at the picture they had taken of him the day at the strip club. "Listen, I know everybody taking this to heart, but I want y'all to remember that this is all part of the game. You win some and you lose some. Its shit like this that builds a bond with the ones you close with and it helps build character. That's why I tell y'all to stay sober and clear minded at all times and of the people you dealing with. All money ain't good money. You do not have to do business with everybody to get rich. The less you seen the fewer questions you have to answer and the longer you will last. Let me pull y'all coat tail on something."

The year was 1995. Bone Thugs and Harmony was having an after party for their album at Club 9.0 in the Flats. It was Rock Man Man and DJ's last night together. The Feds was following the-three misfits for the last 18 months putting together a solid case that would stick in the sixth circuit Federal District of Courts.

Club 9.0 was filled with some of the finest players in the 90's era. The gold diggers was out looking their best. Rock knew the FEDS had followed him to the club that night and knew who the agent was. He walked to the bar. He told the bartender to send the two white men sitting in the corner of the club dressed in plain street clothes a bottle of Moet apiece.

When the music went off the crowd started.

"Mo thugs ... Mo thugs."

"Buck ... Buck ... Buck ... Buck." It was a Waste-Land saying.

Rock and Man-Man had their middle fingers up in the direction of the two federal agents screaming.

"Mo drugs ... Mo drugs!"

Man Man through ten grand in one of the agent's face. The next morning FEDS had conducted a sweep. DJ received twenty years. Rock and Man-Man ended up cooperating for the FEDS. Nobody has seen them since that night.

"What we going to do about this shit! Big Mike is dead!" PW was talking like a drunk.

"We paid them niggas a half a mill ticket and don't know who the fuck they are! One of them niggas could walk past us right now and we would not even know. This shit just ain't adding up!" Pete said looking out the window.

Ty time was getting thin with Deon. He had two weeks to get another control buy from him. Deon had no clue that Ty would do him in. It was his family who took him in and treated him like family.

Two Internal Affairs agents entered the small room inside the Federal building in downtown Cleveland. Officer Dixon was irritated when he seen the two agents entered through the door. Letting out a deep breath he said, "I don't have time for this!" Before the agents could even speak.

"I see you have that cast off your leg." One of the agents said. Officer Dixon did not respond.

"Where is your partner?"

"I don't know where he is, I'm not his babysitter!"

"Oh you a little uptight!" He said grabbing the bottom of Officer Dixon's ear lobe.

"Well we want you to take a look at something." He said throwing a brown envelope on the table.

"What's this?"

"You tell me!" One of the agents as the two agents exited the room.

Officer Dixon was all alone in the room. He stared at the envelope for about two minutes before he decided to open the envelope.

Officer Hill was sitting inside his squad car talking on the phone with the African he had been supplying kilos of heroine to, when the two internal affairs agents knock on his window.

Officer Dixon could not believe what he was seeing. The pictures inside the envelope where pictures of his partner stuffing money inside his pockets. There was even a picture of him with a small bag. The Internal Affairs agents had even took a few picture of him smashing his head through the window. The last picture was of him when he walked in the room.

"Don't think you're going to get away with this!"
One of the Internal Affairs agents said lighting his cigar.

"Officer I have no idea what you two are talking
about." He said starting the police car.

"Time is not on your side, this we all know."

Backing out the parking spot he almost ran one of
the Internal Affairs agents over.

"You are going down asshole!" He said spitting to
the ground. Taking the cigar from his mouth.

Ox and Starr where seating five rows back from
the stage, watching D.L Hughley live. Pete was sitting in
the upper level of the State Theater, so he could keep a
close eye on Ox. He had to admit it, Ox was a smooth
individual. Pete blazed up a haze blunt, hearing an
unfamiliar voice.

"Aye young blood, you got some more of that you
smoking on?" The unfamiliar voice said tapping Pete on
the shoulder. Pete turned around to meet the voice that
took him out his zone. He was blinded from the
diamonds inside the piece that hung from his platinum
chain.

"I only have a fifty sack left. You can get it if you
want to."

"Hell yea I want it. That's all we smoke in
Dayton." The out of towner said.

Pete took a look back at Starr, then back at the out of towner. He could tell he was not from the city just by the way he talked.

"Here hit it!" Pete said passing him the blunt. He had two high yellow females with him well put together. One of the ladies was laughing at the joke the comedian had said. Pete was focusing on how to get the chain from around his neck. He coughed from the strength of the haze, pulling a fresh hundred dollar bill.

"You got change young blood?"

Bud, Larry and Trina set inside Bud's building with the contractors, going over the floor plan to his shop. The extra money from the bank lick came in handy. It was enough to bring his vision to life.

"This section of the shop I would like to have two nail techs and three hair stylists. This section I want it just appointments. The floor I would like it to look just like the Boston Celtics basketball court. A flat screen in each barber station and a laptop."

Trina set back and admired how well put together Bud was. How he could bring his vision to life. It turned her on the more he talked. She loved the way the wool and cashmere sweater complimented his wide frame. Larry stepped outside to get some fresh air, observing the condition of the tableau. It was a nice metropolitan. The shop was in walking distance from the West 28th projects and Club Motta. Lorain Avenue was only a few stoplights away. A soul food cafe sat across the street.

The total came up to sixty grand to get the shop the way he wanted it. Giving the subcontractor fifteen grand to get started.

Bruh Man from the fifth floor, put your hands together!

The liquor that Ox had consumed had him feeling nice. Pete had never witnessed Starr at work.

"Excuse me ladies I have to go to the rest room!" He said zooming passed the onlookers.

Pete heard the voice of the out of Towner.

"Whoa them hot wings got my ass burning" Squatting over the toilet. He had sweat beads running down his nose. Pete cocked his glock before entering the restroom.

It was an old white man drying his hands under the electric hand dryer. Seeing it was only one person in the stalls it had to be the out of Towner. He was in the last stall. Pete could see his bubble gum gators.

"Starr I have to use the bathroom real quick."

"All shit! Where you going nigga? Trying to go and call yo girlfriend!" The comedian said, "Put the spotlight on this nigga!" The crowd was in laughter.

"Boy you look like your mother was on her period when she had you!"

Just as the out of Towner was whooping his ass, Pete kicked the stall door open. Forcing the door to collide with his face.

"Yo what the fuck wrong with you nigga!" He said looking up at an invulnerable Pete.

"Shut yo bitch as up. Let me get this!" He said snatching the chain from around his neck. He hit him over the head repeatedly with his glock.

"I'm going to teach you out of town niggas bout coming up here flossin like something sweet. Nigga, matter fact where that sack I sold you?"

"Help! Somebody help me!"

The more he yelled the harder Pete hit him. Pete ripped his pockets off before heading for the door. Ox opened the door and bumped into Pete.

"Damn nigga say excuse me!" Ox said in an inebriated tone of voice as he looked Pete up and down.

Seeing Ox face Pete tensed up.

"Or what Ox?" Pete stepped closer to Ox. The two were now face to face. Pete hearing the out of towner yelling, he humble himself and exited the building. Ox was appalled that a complete stranger knew his name. Entering the bathroom he heard a low pitched voice.

"Somebody help me!" He walked to the stall where the voice was coming from. He was taken aback seeing a helpless individual pleading for a helping hand. Ox had to hold his breath from the strong smell of shit that filled the stall. He had shit all over his leg and hands.

"Man what happened to you?"

"Some lil' nigga just robbed me!" He said trying to get to his feet.

Ox felt it was kind of strange for somebody to get robbed at a comedy show. Sitting down in his seat. He had a confused look on his face.

"Boy what the hell wrong with you? Look like you seen a ghost!"

"I'm cool. Over the past few weeks I been seeing some crazy shit. I gets to the bathroom and on the way in some nigga had the nerve to bump into me. What was so crazy, the lil' nigga knew my name. Once I get in the bathroom some old head talking about he just got robbed!"

"What bathroom?"

"The one outside in the hallway."

"Yea right!"

"I'm dead ass serious. Then last week I'm riding down 105th St, I see some crazy ass niggas shooting it out with the police in front of the bank!" Starr took a hard swallow.

Tone and Lamika had been shopping all day. He was a little skeptical about what he was about to tell her.

"When was the last time you talked to your brother?"

"Mmm … Since the funeral."

"Next time you talk to him tell em to get at me, I might have something he looking for."

"What the hell you talking about?"

"Forget trying to know what I'm talking about. Just tell him to get at me when
he get a chance." Lamika was not feeling Tone since her and Ty had been seeing each other.

"I can't believe that nigga had the nerve to tell me excuse you. Like I'm something sweet. I can't wait to see that nigga on the rebound." Pete said talking out loud counting the ten grand he just took from the out of towner. Pete was damn near in tears when he seen the out of towner being attended to his all-white H2 Hummer by the police.

Chapter Eighteen

Go Hard or Go Home

The three hustlers were sitting inside Bud's shop talking about how Big Mike got killed. PW spoke, "Something has to shake. We can't let shit like this ride."

Pete was taking Big Mike death kind of hard.

"One thing I just thought about he did not have on his ring. He never took that ring off. That ring Lil' June Bug had on the night he was killed leaving the club, when they was younger." Larry stated.

Pete left the building. He pulled off the traffic light on west 85th switched from yellow to red, trying to beat the light. He never saw the traffic cop under the bridge. Hearing the police sirens he pulled over.

"Fuck they want!"

An overweight cop exited out the squad car. He spit a glob of brown mud from his mouth as he pulled his pants up higher than fitted. He walked with alertness on the two door SUV. One hand was on his weapon inside his holster, the other hand was wrapped around the metal flash light.

"I need to see your license and registration please." He said flashing the light in Pete's face.

"Want you take that bright as light out of my face like that!" He said handing the officer the information he asked for.

"Wait right here."

Ox left Starr in the kitchen cooking fried perch and cheese eggs, while he was in the garage counting his last fifty bricks. This was his last run before he let Tone hold down the mound.

Starr heard someone knocking at the front door.

"Ox somebody at the door?"

"What you telling me for, answer it!"

"Your name came back clean, but your truck was identified in a robbery in Akron Ohio. He called for backup. Four police cars hit the scene within five minutes.

"Fuck you talking about a robbery?"

"Sir we do not want any trouble. Just do as you were told and step out of the vehicle!" Pete was taking into proprietorship and placed in cell 18 inside the Justice center.

Starr opened the door without even looking.

"Tone ... Peaches!" They said at the same time. They both stood there lost for words in a discomforting moment. Starr broke the tense air.

"He in the garage."

Looking at her ass jiggle back and forth inside her Baby Phat boy shorts. Tone thought to himself, *I wouldn't mind having a shot of that pussy.*

He walked into the garage finding Ox sitting inside his 69 Chevy Camaro.

"I see you got fresh meat walking around." He was feeling some kind of way knowing how Pete used Peaches to hit licks.

"Yea that's ole girl I been telling you about."

"Starr ha." He said with disappointment in his voice.

"You act like you know shorty." Starr walked in just in time.

"Ox baby your food is ready. I made a plate for your friend. How come you didn't introduce me to your friend? He looks kind of young to be hanging out with someone as grown as you." Starr said with a deceitful look.

"Oh this my partner Tone, I been telling you about and this is Starr."

"Nice to meet you." Starr said sticking her hand out to embrace Tone's.

Tone was boiling hot on the inside, looking at Peaches playing her role. She knew Tone wanted to fuck her ever since the night at the hotel in Buffalo when he seen her naked in the room. Time was running out. Especially since her cover was blown. It was only a matter of time before Tone told him the truth about who she really is. Turning the shower on she forgot there was no clean towels in the bathroom. Hearing Ox and Tone talking she took it upon herself to be nosey.

Inside his walk in closet she found two army bags filled with money. All hundreds. Hearing Ox coming up the steps. He heard the shower running and he thought she was in the bathroom.

"I thought you was in the shower."

"I was about to get in, but I forgot there were no clean towels."

"Oh shit I forgot. Look in the other closet on the first shelf on the left."

Soon as Starr got out the shower her phone started ringing. Still with the towel around her, she answered.

"You have a collect call from Pete to accept press five."

"Pete what the hell you doing in jail?"

"I will tell you when you come bail me out."

"How much is your bond?"

"A stack!"

"Fuck you done did now Pete? You always in some shit. I will have Ox bring me down there when he drop me off."

Looking out the window at Ox and Tone in the driveway brought her back to reality.

Tone pulled off with his mind all over the place. *How the fuck did Peaches get in good with Ox like that without me noticing.* He was trying to figure out how much she knew about him. *That's why Lamika been acting funny. Peaches done filled her head with that bull shit.*

Starr was standing in the doorway when he came back in the house.

"Ox can you do me a favor until you take me home?"

"What's that?

"My brother got into some trouble. Can you take-me to the Justice-Center so I can pay his bail?"

"How much is it?"

"A thousand dollars."

"Fuck he did?"

"I don't know, he always in some trouble."

PW was about to get on the freeway when he seen a for sale sign on a building on West Road with a number on it. He called the number ASAP.

"Hello, I'm calling in regards to a building you have for sale."

"May I ask who is this calling?"

"Yea this is Michael. If you do not mind me asking. Who am I speaking with?" "This is the owner of the building, my name is Mr. Ellington."

"I'm interested in looking at the building whenever you have time. When will it be a good day for you?"

"How about 12:00 Friday afternoon."

"That's cool with me."

Bud and Larry was locking up the shop when Shanell called and invited him to dinner with her and her sister at Lancer's restaurant.

"I can make that happen, I got my uncle with me. I should be there in about 20 minutes."

Bud and Larry entered the bar and lounge and took a seat at the small bar. The Cavs was playing the Heat on TNT when Bud remembered he had a few tickets for the up and coming game with King James and Kobe Bryant. A waiter tapped Bud on the shoulder. Pointing in the direction Shanell and her sister was sitting in.

"I did not even know you were here."

"How rude of you Bud, not introducing me to your friend's sister." He said extending his hand out to shake Shanell's sister's hand.

"I'm Larry!"

"My name is Tammy. Nice to meet you."

After a few drinks got tossed back, the two sisters were more comfortable. This was right up Larry's alley. He was in Mack mode.

"Say lil' ma won't you stand up and let me see that shape. Whoo Wee, with all that ass a nigga will never be broke!"

Pete was being ruffian by Cleveland Police and Two Akron detective.

"Look asshole we know for sure that the truck you was in was used in a robbery a few months back, that involved a seventeen year old getting shot in the back and two teenaged females being badly beaten."

The Cleveland detective through a few photos on the table. Pete was actually looking at pictures from the bank robbery. The good thing about the pictures everybody had on a mask.

"This bank robbery took the lives of two off duty police officers."

"Fuck I look like doing your job for you! Get me back to my cell!"

"It's only going to be a matter of time before the ceiling come crashing down on you and your team!"

Once Pete was back inside his cell he called officer Bullet by his first name. "Before I rat on anybody you will be on my payroll nigga!"

Starr had been standing in line for an hour and half a before she was able to pay Pete's bond.

"He should be out within the next few hours." The feminine male clerk said.
Starr made it back to the truck just in time. A traffic cop pulled up behind Ox's truck hitting the loud speaker.

"Move it!"

"What they say?"

"He should be out in a few hours."

"I wish I had some body to bail me out. My family moved to Atlanta when I was twelve. I been in the streets ever since."

"Take me home Ox, I need to get some rest."

179

"Where that's at?"

"Just drive!" Starr was mentally tired so much had been going on, she had not made any time for herself. They pulled into the complex parking lot. He had a quick flashback. Seeing the same Lexus truck that was parked behind his car the night of the New Year's party.

"Come in." Ox left the truck running. He entered her apartment. He was impressed with the lavish interior design.

"I will be right back." Observing the interior of her home. Looking around he could tell she did not live by herself.

"Thanks for loaning me that money." She said handing him ten hundred dollar bills.

"What's this? Girl you trippin. You don't have to give me that money back. I don't care how much his bond is, I won't let nobody sit in jail. Matter of fact, soon as he touch down, I want to meet him, I got something for him. I'm going to make sure he gets on his feet."

Starr was going to introduce him to Pete aright. Soon as he pulled out the complex Tone called him.

"C-Lo, you see Manny hit Steve with that lock in the sock last night in the TV room?" Sunshine and C-Lo worked inside the, commissary warehouse. They were pulling an order for the education department. Mr. Vails had ordered five boxes of tissue and two cases of envelopes. C-Lo was waiting on a package from Barnes and Noble bookstore.

The commissary warehouse is where everything packaged entering the prison go before it enters the institution. The packages are ran through a scanner, making sure no contraband are in the packages.

"Tone what up?"

"Turn the music down. I have something to tell you."

"What the business bruh?"

"You remember when I was telling you about my mans nem from cross town?"

"Yea I remember."

"You fucking with his main squeeze bruh."

"Who fucking with who squeeze?"

"You is!" He said hopping out his all-white 745 BMW.

"You talking about Starr?"

"Fucking fool her name is Peaches. She mess with my girl's brother. His name is Pete."

"I just took her to pay her brother bail."

"Nigga she ain't got no brother. The nigga you just bailed out was Pete. Slim is a certified jack boy. He good at what he do. Knowing him he using Peaches to get close to you. She do hair, got a lil' apartment on 71st and Wade Park inside the complex."

"That's where I dropped her off at."

"Boy you slipping hard."

Ox cut him off in mid-sentence.

"I'ma hit you back bruh!"

"UPS!" The CO yelled from the loading dock. When the CO ran the boxes through the scanner CO Vails told Sunshine to bring his order to the scanner. CO Rolloff was C-Lo's and Sunshine's boss. CO Vails was standing behind the two inmates.

"Run that package back through. Something do not look right. Stop the machine!" CO Vails opened the small box.

Inside the small box was six hard back books from Barnes and Noble bookstore, without an inmate name. It was addressed to the education department.

"These books just do not look right to me!" CO Vails said as he tossed one of the books to Officer Roll off. Rolloff did not give a damn. He was a laid back CO who let the inmates do them. He was to retire in three months.

"Bingo!" CO Vails said. Finding two small cell phones inside the fold of the books. C-Lo was mad as hell he was going to sell each phone for a thousand dollars apiece.

Chapter Nineteen

"Bud I need you to come pick me up."

"Pick you up from where?"

"I'm sitting outside the Justice Center."

"Fuck you doing down their?

"Long story bruh. I will fill you in when you get here. Pick Peaches up before you come."

"What side you on?"

"I'm on the side facing the Browns Stadium."

Officer Hill and two other federal agents where sitting inside Agent Smith's living room on the outskirts of PA. Agent Smith had retired six months ago. He was the one who turned Officer Hill and his comrades out. They were all involved in illicit activities.

"So how's life been going for an old culprit?" Agent Lloyd stated opening a cold Millers Lite beer.

"I can't complain. I miss the action some days, but I enjoy the wealth from the action."

"Aye Steve!" He said calling Officer Hill by his first name.

"I heard you done got yourself in some serious shit being greedy. I told you when we first started, you never know who is watching the score. Unfortunately for you Internal Affairs happened to be watching your score."

Officer Hill walked up behind the retired agent, who was sitting inside a reposeful leather recliner chair. Bending down so he could hear him clearly.

"Everybody could not retire with two million dollars in drug money. Let me remind you, you barely made it out your damn self thanks to the help of us!" Smith was feeling the cold vibe from the malice inside Officer Hill's voice. Knowing it was his two million dollars that brought the three dirty agents his way.

"What brings you scumbags this way? It's been 18 months since I last seen any of you."

"When have we ever made a home visit and leave empty handed?" Agent Black said pulling out his glock .40 placing it on his lap sitting directly across from Smith.

Ty stumbled into Deon inside Church's Chicken.

"Thought that was you. I been looking for you bruh. Lost my phone with your number in it. Shit still in motion, it's all love get at me." Deon said exiting the franchise.

"What you was in jail for Pete?" Bud asked before he could get content in the back seat.

"Before you flip out let me explain. Me and Nutt was bending corners one day we ended up at the mall in Akron. Nutt said he remember where his peeps had took him to get some weed one time. Anyway we hit the spot for some weed and some money. On the way out I guess somebody got the license plate number to my truck. I got pulled over leaving from your shop that night running a red light. Some fat cop ran my truck and said it was used in a robbery. They kept me for 72 hours. They showed me some pictures from the bank lick. He said he was going to be watching me closely."

"So what happened to the weed? What the hell you been out here doing?"

"Bruh for the past six months I been on a tear. I have not spent a dime or touched any of the product from the licks I hit."

"You dirty sons of bitches! Think y'all going to come in here and take my fucking money!"

"Yep and you can't do nothing about it!" Officer Lloyd said hitting Smith with the Taser, leaving him slumped in his chair from the electric currents.

"Sorry it had to be this way!" Officer Hill said spitting in his face.

"It was me who helped keep you on the force ten years ago. This is how you repay me!" Smith said out of breath from the taster gun.

Boom Boom! Officer Black hit Smith with two dome shots.

"Get the shovel so we can dig this money up out the floor."

"Man turn his old as around I don't want him looking at me while I'm trying to focus!"

"You was the one who shot him, now he can't look at you!"

Chapter Twenty

Bud pulled into Pete's and Peaches' driveway of their residential home in Uppety Heights. Sitting in the driveway, Pete gave Bud the rundown about Tone and Ox.

"If anything happens to me you and Peaches will know what happened and what to do. This is a lick I cannot pass up bruh!"

They entered their place of living. Pete had Peaches run him some bathwater. While taking a bath, Peaches washed his back. She filled him in on what happened with her and Tone when he came by Ox's house. She also told him about the two bags of money she seen in the closet.

"I seen him counting out fifty bricks that Tone was to pick up. He left them in the garage inside his old school back seat. Whatever you plan on doing you need to make your move before it is too late!"

Pete had his mind made up. Peaches made extra copies of all Ox's keys to his house. She even knew the security code to his alarm system.

"I put the extra set of keys to his house on the table in the living room. His two pit bulls Salt and Pepper will be at the vet for the next few days. They go once a year. Make sure when you enter his house, you come through the second car garage. Wait after ten o'clock. He got somebody that comes by and cut the grass and water his flowers. I emptied all the bullets out of all his guns that was laying out around the house that I could find.

Ty and Officer Dixon were in position inside an old Wonder Bread truck when Deon picked up his cell phone.

"What's good young Ty? Come to the spot. This was the control buy Officer Dixon needed to crack this case wide open. He parked three streets over from the location he was told to come. Ty called him again before getting in the car with Officer Hill.

When Ty entered the house, he was introduced to the same individual he previously done business with inside the bank. Deon was in the basement watching the five TV monitors that was observing the areas he had cameras positioned in. He was focusing on the middle aged white driver that Ty was in the car with. Looking at the screen that showed Ty and Rodney, he was paying extra attention to Ty's body language.

He was talking to Rodney through the earpiece.

"Aye yo tell that nigga ain't nothing poppin. Something don't look right outside!"

Putting two and two together Ty was the only new customer he started doing business with over the past year. He hated to admit it but Ty was working for the FBI.

Officer Dixon could not believe what he was hearing. Ty came back to the vehicle to find Officer Hill writing down the address to the house he just exited out of. The driver of the Dodge Ram truck could not wait to put Ty out of his misery, seeing him get out of the car with a white unknown man then get back in the Wonder Bread truck.

Tone was ready to take over the city streets he loved. He pulled up on Young Smack, his closet childhood friend.

"Get in Smack!" He said letting the window down.

"What's good bruh?" Smack asked placing his pistol on his lap.

"Man I'm tired as hell. I been out here all night trying to bounce back."

"What happen?"

"I fell asleep over crackhead Jean's house the other day. One of them bitches took my whole bag of dope. Shit fucked me up bruh."

"Look don't even trip. Look on the back seat, I got something for you. That's you bruh. Get right. Bring me back fifteen stacks. Take your time. It's more where that came from. Told you once I get right I got you. My word is all I have."

Chapter Twenty-One

Pete went to K-Mart shopping store to attain everything he needed to hit the lick on Ox. Just thinking about the money and the dope he would walk away with, made his heart skip a beat. This was the big takeout he had been waiting for.

Pete, Tone and Lamika where sitting at the kitchen table. Tone felt uncomfortable being around Pete, knowing that Peaches was in good
with Ox.

"What up Tone. I see yo mans treating you good." Pete said.

"Pete Tone said he wanted to talk to you about something." Lamika said while looking at Tome and talking to Pete.

"What you finally trying to break bread nigga. Other than talking to Pete that ain't shit to talk about!" Lamika excused herself.

"Pete what you got against me. I don't know."

I ain't did shit to you. I been had work from day one. You and PW was fucken' with Big Mike so I never stepped on his toes. I'm sorry to hear what happened to him, my heart goes out to him. Like I was telling your sister if you wanted to talk business then we can come to an agreement to where me and you can make a nice piece of money. I'm willing to let you get on for fifteen a key. That's the best I can do."

"Nigga you got some kind of nerve! Fuck you think you talking to. Nigga you should of been broke bread with us and Big Mike from day one. We never held nothing back from you. I don't want shit from you nigga! Yo day go come!"

Meanwhile

Peaches was styling her toenails when Pete came through the door. He walked into the bedroom without acknowledging her. He was counting every dime he had from the bank robbery and the licks he had hit over the past few months. He was sitting on four hundred and sixty thousand dollars, fifty pounds of weed, seven keys and an iced out chain. He called Peaches into the room.

"What Pete, you know my toenails wet!"

"Girl bring yo ass in here!" He said in a virile tone of voice.

"Take this ten grand downtown in the morning and give it to Mike's old lawyer. Bud gone call you in a few weeks with 125 grand, you and my sister split it down the middle."

Pete called Bud and told him to meet him on the Deuces. When Pete pulled in the driveway of Granny D's house, her and bud was on the porch talking about her moving back to down south

Pete kissed her on the forehead. Handing her a bag filled with all the money from the bank lick.

"Here this is for you. Don't open it. Wait until you get in the house. I been saving this money for a while. I want to tell you thanks for everything and taking me and my sister in. I love you Granny D. He hugged her able body.

"Bud let me talk to you for a second."

Officer Bullet was sitting inside an unmarked SUV watching Pete and Bud from 81st street through the field when his cell phone rang. It was the detective from Akron informing him that he had a witness from the robbery a few months back.

"I'm pulling in the garage of the Justice Center right now." The Akron Detective said.

"Look bruh you all I got. Give these seven keys to PW.

Tell him he ole me 17.5 a stack. All I got is fifty pounds for you, you ole me five hundred a pound. When y'all get done call and give the money to Peaches.

Chapter Twenty-Two

Bud, his son and Larry were sitting five rows back from the Cleveland Cavaliers bench LeBron James had subbed back into the game. They were down eight points to the visiting Lakers. Sitting next to Bud was a confident thirty year old male who seem to have a neutral relationship with a few of the Cavs players.

King James hit a deep three in the defender's face to cut the deficit to five. The crowd was becoming more in tuned with the game. With one minute and forty eight seconds left the third quarter.

"Yo Boobie tell the coach to put you in the game!" The spectator sitting next to Bud yelled out.

Derrick Fisher passed the ball off to Kobe Bryant. King James deflected the ball into the back court. The younger James shuffled to the ball gaining momentum all in one motion cocking his arm back at the height of his elevation, slamming the basketball with great force. The crowd was electrified. Phil Jackson called a twenty second time out. King James was trying to get the crowd into it by waving his hands up and down. The cheerleaders were throwing small basketballs into the stands. Bud's son had just missed one of the small basketballs. Bud was trying to get the attention of the cheerleaders when their section came on the jumbo Tron. One of the cheerleaders threw the last ball in the direction they were sitting in. Hitting the hand of a fan sitting in front of them then landing in the lap of the spectator sitting next to them.

"Yo cuzzo give this to your son!"

"Good looking out Bruh!"

"Defense! Defense! Defense!" The crowd was squawking when Kobe beat the twenty-four second shot clock with an Off balance shot through the lane. To quiet the crowd.

"Yo fam, if you don't mind me asking, what's your name?" Bud asked.

"They call me Greedy." He said extending his hand.

"Bud."

Greedy was a real observant cat. He respected dudes who took care of their kids. That meant a lot to him. He saw Bud's son was well dressed and he noticed the diamond earrings. He was looking Bud up and down. He could tell Bud was in the dope game.

"Yo fam I appreciate what you did."

"Don't trip that's what real niggas do. Look bruh I know how much the small things mean to a child. How old is he?"

"Eighteen months. This my lil' partner." King James split two defenders in the lane leaving his feet making body contact from Bynum the Lakers seven foot center. James finger was rolling with his left hand. The game official blew his whistle just as the ball was going through the bottom of the net.

"Where you from?"

"I'm from 79th and Money."

"I know a few people down that way. So what you into if you don't mind me asking." Looking over at Larry. He hesitated for a second before Larry nodded his head.

"I cut hair and sell a lil' weed here and there."

"Look I'm going to do you a favor. I like your style. Here's my card. Call me when you get a chance."

Tone had sold fifteen bricks in two days. He was in the car with his mother going to visit his older brother C-Lo. He pulled out his cell phone and dialed Ox's number.

"Yo."

"Ox what's good big bruh long time no hear from."

"I can't call it!"

"We about an hour away from the spot me and mom dukes. Should be back around seven or eight tonight."

"Tell him I put some more money on his account Wednesday."

C-Lo was surprised to see the rapid growth physically from his younger brother. Tone hugged him like a father would do his son.

"I see the streets does a body good." Playfully hitting Tone in the chest. The last time Tone came to visit his older brother was almost two years ago.

"Ma what's wrong, baby girl you alright?"

"I just have something I want to tell y'all."

"Tell us what."

A small tear formed in the corner of her right eye.

"I'm dying! I have full blown breast cancer!"

When Bud and Larry pulled inside Granny D's driveway, PW was having a conversation with Nicole, a female from around the way.

"Answer the phone when I call you later, I'm trying to get up in that later on."

"Boy please!" Nicole said walking away blushing.

"I told you about that nigga. He got pussy on his mind more than money."

"In a minute them hoes gone think you tricking."

"Damn nigga you slammed my door like you crazy!" Bud said.

"Aye Bud!" PW yelled out.

"If you ain't busy I want you to ride somewhere with me."

Just as he was getting in the car with PW Tammy pulled up picking Larry up. PW tried to pass Bud the blunt he declined.

"Damn nigga you ain't smoking no more?"

"It ain't that, a nigga just focused right now. Oh yea before I forget, Pete told me to give you something. You have to come by the crib and get it doe."

"What the hell Pete on?"

"I don't know bruh, I just got something he told me to give you." He said in a dry tone of voice. PW pulled up in the parking lot of a vacant building.

"PW where the hell you got me at?"

"Relax bruh. This me. Let me show you the inside. I'ma turn it into a one stop auto body shop.

"That's what the fuck I'm talking about bruh. Big boy business move my nigga. You worked hard for it, you deserve it. Whatever you need let me know."

Larry was sitting on the couch when Tammy's brother Brain walked in. Being disrespectful he didn't say shit to Larry.

"Disrespectful ass lil' niggas these days." He said turning the TV to CNN news. When Tammy and her brother entered the living room Larry stood up sizing Brain up.

"Larry this is my brother Brain."

"What up young blood." Larry said extending his hand.

"That's a nice ring."

"Yea I came up on this a few months ago. Some phatt ass nigga trying to tax us like something was sweet!"

"Oh yea that's how you get down young blood."

"You know sometimes you have to do what you have to do to make ends meet out here!" Larry was steaming hot on the inside.

Officer Bullet entered the office. Sitting in the cold dull and moist room was the detective from Akron, Ohio and a key witness in the robbery case with Pete.

Ron-Ron was having a warm cup of tea when Officer Bullet took a seat on the edge of the table.

"So let me get this clear. You said it was two masked gunmen who invaded your place of living and robbed you at gunpoint. Is that correct?"

"Yes!"

"Now if they were masked up how did you see anybody face?"

"After they took off running to their getaway vehicle the driver of the truck took of-his mask before getting into the truck."

"We have a description of the truck can you describe it to us?"

"It was a two door black Yukon GMC truck."

"If I show you some pictures, can you identify the man who invaded your home?" He said showing Ron-Ron a lineup of criminals they arrested in the past two months.

"Go back! Naw not that page, the page before that one, that's him right there!"

Ty had just flew in from Boston testifying in his first case as a confidential informant. Suga Ray was a big time drug lord who sold Ty five keys of cocaine three years ago. When Suga Ray seen Ty walk through the doors of the courtroom his heart fell through his stomach.

Ty received fifty thousand, a new house and a S550 Benz for his cooperation. Suga Ray, the Boston drug lord, was handed a thirty five year sentence.

Lamika positioned her 36" butt inside the butter scotch leather seats of Ty's S550. The driver of the dodge ram had been tailing Ty for the last two hours. Staying six car links back.

You have a collect call from C-Lo press five to accept. If you wish to refuse this call hang up to block all calls press seven now.

"What's good bruh?"

"You sound good, how did your visit go?"

"It was cool mom dukes talking about she got breast cancer and shit, when she told me that it fucked my whole visit up."

"Sorry to hear that bruh. You know I'm always here fo you bruh, no matter what happens. Next week my lawyer will be coming to see you to fill you in on what I was talking about in that letter I sent you a few weeks back. I told you from day one I was going to stay true to my word."

"It's all on your lil' brother. I can't get no bigger. I got a house out in Florida. The club doing numbers. I'm out bruh."

"Damn dawg you just go up and leave like that?"
You have one minute left remaining on this call.
"I'm going to hit you back sometime next week."

Ty pulled his luxury sedan inside the Marathon gas station on 185th and S.Waterloo just south of St.Clair Avenue .

"You want something out of here?" Ty asked Lamika.

"Yea bring me a pack of Mambas."

"That's all you want?" He asked opening his door. Before he could step foot on the pavement, the driver of the Dodge Ram truck blocked him off, crippling his movements.

Matt rose up from the bed of the pickup with a Strya AVG Pullpop 308 fully automatic with a reversed stick.

"You rat ass nigga" He rained hot bullets in the driver's side of the car. Screams could be heard from the customers and humanity. The tan metal was no match for the 308 bullets.

Ty tried to allude the rain of bullets. Vaulting over Lamika to open

the passenger's door. The force from the weapon was too much for the both of them.

Lamika suffered two brutal wounds. One to the left hip and the other in the leg. Ty laid lifeless on top of Lamika.

PW answered Bud's ringing cell phone.

"Where you at?" A histrionic voice asked.

"Larry calm down this PW.

"Tell Bud to meet me at Gordan Park in twenty minutes!"

Printed in Great Britain
by Amazon

69140010R00119